ABENAKI CAPTIVE

ABENAKI CAPTIVE

by Muriel L. Dubois

Carolrhoda Books, Inc./Minneapolis

Adventures in Time Books

Note to Readers
A glossary of Abenaki words and names appears on page 174.

LIBRARY OF CONGRESS CATALOGING-IN PUBLICATION DATA
Dubois, Muriel L.
  Abenaki Captive / by Muriel L. Dubois; art by Susan Fair Lieber.
    p. cm.
  Summary: In 1752, eighteen-year-old Abenaki warrior Ogistin is present when a band of his people capture an English trapper, John Stark, and as Stark is carried into captivity in Canada a bond of hate and competition develops between him and Ogistin.
    ISBN 0-87614-753-8—ISBN 0-87614-601-9 (pbk.)
    1. Stark, John 1728–1822—Juvenile fiction. 2. Abenaki Indians—Captivities—Juvenile fiction. [1. Stark, John, 1728–1822—Fiction. 2. Abenaki Indians—Captivities—Fiction. 3. Indians of North America—Canada—Captivities—Fiction. 4. Canada—Fiction.]
  I. Title.
PZ7.D85225Ab 1993

Manufactured in the United States of America

1 2 3 4 5 6 I / BP 99 98 97 96 95 94

*To Dick, for nineteen years of encouragement;
and for Aimée, Craig, and Elise,
who make our love complete.*

Historical Note

For thousands of years, the Wabanaki, or People of the Dawnland, lived in the northeastern part of the North American continent. The Wabanaki, which included the Abenaki, Micmac, Pennacook, Penobscot, Sokoki, and others, settled from the Merrimack River Valley north to Nova Scotia, and from the Champlain Valley to the Atlantic coast.

The Wabanaki did some farming, but they were especially known as excellent hunters and fishers. Each Wabanaki band spoke variations of the same language and had its own form of government and religion.

When European colonists began to settle in North America, the lives of the Wabanaki were changed drastically. Not only did European settlers introduce new tools and weapons, they also carried diseases with them. The Wabanaki had no defenses against illnesses such as measles and smallpox. Hundreds of people died in every band.

The colonists started claiming land that had been homelands of the Wabanaki nation, trying to force the Wabanaki out. The weakened Wabanaki bands sometimes fought the colonists. Other times, they agreed on treaties to share the land, for they did not believe anyone could own it. Land was meant to be used by all.

By the mid-1600s, the French and British colonists fought among themselves over the land. The Wabanaki sided with the French. The Wabanaki's long-standing enemies, the Iroquois, fought alongside the British.

Over the hundred years of fighting, many members of Wabanaki bands were left without homes. They headed north and settled in French mission villages. One such village was St. Francis. The villagers combined their traditions, and adopted French and Catholic customs that suited them. By the early 1700s, this Wabanaki band was called the St. Francis Abenaki by both the villagers and colonists.

The colonists called the villagers and other native nations "Indians" (though the name is not accurate), and the St. Francis Abenaki referred to the English settlers as "Pastoni." This comes from the French term "Bastonnais," meaning "from Boston." The Abenaki believed all the English colonists were under the control of the Royal Governor of Boston.

In the 1700s, scalping was a common practice

among both the native warriors and colonial soldiers. Native historians, archaeologists, and anthropologists disagree about how scalping began. Many say scalping was begun by European soldiers. They scalped their enemies and paid their Native American allies money for each enemy scalp taken so they could count the number of enemy killed.

Other scholars say there is also evidence that scalping was an ancient custom among the Wabanaki. If even a small part of an enemy's scalp was taken, a warrior controlled the enemy's soul. By the mid-1700s, scalping was probably done for both reasons.

The year 1752 was a time of peace between wars. France claimed what is now Canada. England claimed the land that now makes up the New England states. The Royal Governor of Boston, however, had agreed to the right of the Abenaki to hunt in the region south of St. Francis to the White Hills by providing them with a deed.

In the spring of 1752, ten Abenaki hunters came upon four Pastoni trappers taking game on these lands. Some of the English trappers were captured. *Abenaki Captive* is based on the historical accounts of this event.

A Few Words from the Author

One cold, gray October morning, I walked across the village green of Odanak, Quebec, to the bluff that overlooks the St. Francis River. Small bushes and trees sporting brightly colored leaves covered the hillside. The river below was moving quickly, and its rushing drowned out the sounds of the occasional passing car.

I had come to Odanak to do some research. This modern Abenaki community is home to approximately three hundred residents, and many work to preserve their native culture, language, and traditions.

A few years earlier, I had read a story about the capture of some New England colonists by a group of Abenaki hunters from this community in 1752. The story had interested me because the colonists had come from Derryfield, New Hampshire—now my hometown of Manchester. Also, Odanak is near the towns in which my French-Canadian grandparents had lived. One of my great-great-grandmothers was Native American. Could she have known or met these people? Could she have been one of them?

Gradually, as I read further, other questions began to form in my mind. Why had the Abenaki captured the English colonists during a supposed time of peace? What was life like for the Abenaki and the colonists? How did this story end?

I spoke with archaeologists, anthropologists, historians, and biologists. I discussed my questions with Abenaki people and others from Odanak. Slowly I learned about what life was like here in 1752.

The village center is still arranged much the way it was then. The Catholic church is the centerpiece, and other buildings surround it in a sort of semicircle, leaving a large open area in front of the church. The doors of the church face the river, for the river was the "main road" of the Abenaki people for centuries.

As I looked down the hillside at the swift-flowing St. Francis River, I thought back to that time two hundred and fifty years earlier, when Odanak was known as St. Francis and the river was called Alsigôtêgok. The wonderful October smells were the same. I closed my eyes, feeling the breeze on my face, and imagined two thirteen-year-old boys scrambling up the hill after dragging ashore their canoe...

Muriel L. Dubois

PART I

Late Autumn, 1747
The Village of St. Francis

Names not in script
are the present names

Quebec

Trois Rivières.

St. François
Odanak

Arsigôtegot
St. Francis
River

MonTréal

St. lawrence River

NEW BRUNSWICK

CANADA   U.S.A.

MAINE

Missisquois
Swanton

NEW YORK

VERMONT   Baker
River

Pemigawassett River

White Hills

Lake Winnepesoga

Rumney.   Lake Winnipesaukee

NEW
HAMPSHIRE   Merrimach River

Derryfield

Rumford.

Concord   Manchester

Dunstable

Albany.   Nashua

Hudson River

Boston.

MASSACHUSETTS

CONNECTICUT

R.I.

N
W   E
S

1752

1
Death of a Warrior

O gistin and Kasko were still laughing as they hauled their canoe ashore. Although they were dressed nearly identically in high winter moccasins and long, leather tunics, Ogistin's clothing was soaked. His straight, loose hair had just begun to dry.

"You should thank me," Kasko said, grabbing his musket and a large goose from the bottom of the canoe. "I probably helped you get the biggest one in the flock."

Just as Ogistin had taken aim, Kasko had nudged his arm so that the shot went wild. Surprisingly, the bullet struck—not the leader, but a gander farther back in formation.

"It only proves that a good hunter's shot always flies true," Ogistin said with a triumphant grin, taking the prize from his friend's hand. Kasko laughed at such a boast and scrambled up the steep bank to the village, Ogistin right behind him.

Kasko reached the top of the bluff first. He grabbed Ogistin's arm and gestured toward the village center. At first, Ogistin didn't understand. He scanned the half-moon of cabins that surrounded the log chapel. People were leaving their work, clustering around a small group of men gathered in front of the church. Ogistin's father, Azô, was talking to the priest, Père Aubery. Beside them, Ogistin's uncle, Plaswa, stood quietly, listening.

Ogistin's stomach tightened. "Why is my uncle here?" he asked Kasko but didn't wait for a reply. The two boys hurried toward the men.

Plaswa had left, just a week before, leading a group of men south to hunt below the White Hills. Ogistin's older brother, Simo, had gone with them. At eighteen summers, he was the youngest of the group. He had shown his ability as a hunter since childhood, helping his father provide for their mother, three sisters, and Ogistin. Simo had also hunted for their grandmother and several others who had no hunters in their family.

This year, Plaswa had invited Simo on the winter hunt. The men left for months, hunting and trapping animals for the thick furs the village depended upon for trade with the French and the English.

So why, Ogistin wondered, as he and Kasko neared the chapel, was Plaswa back so soon after the group's departure?

The boys walked between the neighbors who surrounded Azô, Plaswa, and the priest, and stood respectfully behind the men. Ogistin clenched his teeth, waiting to hear, afraid to know.

"Please consider a Catholic ceremony for your son, Azô," Père Aubery was saying.

Azô replied quietly but firmly. "Simo was a warrior, killed in battle, and will be buried as such, Patlihôz." He turned, not noticing Ogistin at all, and walked toward the family's cabin.

Ogistin and Kasko looked at each other and pushed closer to Plaswa.

"Talk to him, Plaswa," Père Aubery said. The old man held his palms up, imploring. The pose made the priest look like one of the spirit creatures Grandmother told about. His head seemed too large, and his white beard hung in a scraggly mess over his black woolen robe. "The boy needs the prayers and ceremony that will help his journey to heaven."

"Perhaps Azô does not wish to send his son to your French heaven, Patlihôz," Plaswa answered. "My sister's husband will choose for his son." He turned, saw the two boys, and motioned for them to follow him.

Ogistin and Kasko ran to catch up with Plaswa, who was already heading in the same direction as Azô. "Nzasis," Ogistin said to Plaswa. He intended no disrespect by addressing the Chief of the Hunt as "my mother's brother." This was a family matter. "It's true, then. My brother's dead."

"He died bravely, Ogistin." Plaswa paused and put a hand on the boy's shoulder. "We were attacked by Pastoni soldiers. Simo managed to bring down two Pastoni before he was killed." Plaswa turned to enter the cabin. "I must tell your mother now," he said.

The boys stood for a minute, until finally Kasko took the goose Ogistin still gripped in his fist. "I'll take care of it," he said. "You need to help your father." Kasko pulled the goose out of Ogistin's hands and pretended not to notice the extra shine in his friend's eyes. He started to leave but glanced back at Ogistin. "Simo always brought honor to our village."

Ogistin's jaw trembled, and his voice was a hoarse whisper. "Yes, he did." He went into the cabin to join his grieving family.

Simo's body lay near the far wall as it had most evenings when the family slept. His eyes were closed, and someone had covered him with a blanket.

Plaswa was holding Ogistin's mother, O'nis, and whispering to her the same story of Simo's brave death. Ogistin's sisters, Talaz and Agat, wept softly while Mali, the eldest, stood silently above Simo's body. Azô had gone again, no doubt to tell Grandmother and begin preparations for the burial.

Ogistin stood behind Mali and looked down at Simo's quiet face. For a second, he wanted to tell everyone to stop teasing, wanted to pull Simo up by the arm and wrestle with him for frightening him with this ridiculous story. But then Mali knelt and pulled away the blanket that covered their older brother's body.

Most of Simo's left shoulder had been blown away, revealing muscle and bone. Mali gasped and turned away. She dropped the blanket, leaving the wound uncovered.

Ogistin didn't move. Simo had been a tall, strong, handsome man. Ogistin felt his eyes blur and for a moment, his sleeping brother was perfect once again. But when the tears fell, the awful picture became clear.

Ogistin knelt and gently resettled the blanket, leaving two dark tear stains on the cloth. He shook his head. He wouldn't let anyone see him cry.

Mali began to tend to their meal. She whispered a scolding to Agat and Talaz, shaming her younger sisters into helping. No one complained. It was better to work at a time like this.

Even O'nis pushed herself away from Plaswa's arms. Her face seemed older, worn, but there were no more tears. Ogistin marveled at his mother's strength as she reached for cloth rags and water. O'nis would prepare Simo's body for his death journey, just as she had washed him on the day he was born.

Ogistin, too, knew what he could do. He had noticed a large hemlock tree on one of Alsigôtêgok's islands earlier this morning. He and Kasko had admired its size, commenting on the tree's obvious long life. Ogistin would find his father. He felt sure Azô would agree that the bark was thick and wide enough to make the right kind of coffin for a warrior killed in battle.

Père Aubery could not convince Azô to change his mind. By the next evening, Simo's body was placed in the bark coffin. The family provided him with everything he would need on this final journey. Food and weapons were put in the coffin with the body. Ogistin untied the hunting bag that hung from his waist cinch, ready to return it for Simo's use. His father stopped him.

"No, Ogistin. Your brother meant for you to have

it. Mali has made him another. Let that be your sister's gift," Azô told him. "Get some of your best arrows instead."

Plaswa helped Azô wrap the bark around Simo's body and tie the coffin securely with woven rope. Azô, himself, drilled the tiny holes at the top of the coffin, which would let Simo's spirit pass through to the Kingdom of the Great Hunt. O'nis blackened her face and cut her hair, beginning the family's three weeks of mourning.

For three days, the villagers sang the prayers and danced the ancient steps to accompany Simo's spirit during this traveling time. Simo's casket was taken to the highest point in the village to be buried among the ancestors who had made the journey to the Kingdom before him.

After the burial, Ogistin ran down the bluff and jumped into the nearest canoe. He paddled furiously, traveling north, until the early darkness made his trip more difficult. He stopped at one of the small islands that dotted Alsigôtêgok and pulled his canoe ashore. Only then did he notice Kasko, several canoe lengths behind, quietly paddling toward him.

Kasko didn't ask any questions but helped Ogistin gather wood to build a fire.

"I'm staying here tonight," Ogistin said, finally. "I can't stay in the village. Go back if you like."

"Your father knows I'm with you," Kasko said.

The two boys sat side by side, the fire alternately shadowing and lighting their faces.

Kasko lifted a pouch from his shoulder and took out chunks of dried meat, offering some to Ogistin. He chose a small piece and bit into it. "I've been trying to imagine Simo's last moments," he told Kasko.

"The hunting party knew there was a risk," his friend pointed out. "Since the French and Pastoni are at war once again, the Pastoni treat all Abenaki as enemies."

Ogistin let out a breath. "I asked Plaswa if I can go back on the hunt with him, to take Simo's place."

"Will he let you go?" Kasko asked.

"No, he's taking Missal. It's already decided." Ogistin pulled his knees up to his chest. "I can hunt as well as Missal."

Kasko nodded. "You're almost as good as I am." He nudged Ogistin to show that he was teasing. Ogistin smiled. "Grandmother is as good as you are," he teased back.

Ogistin studied the embers of the fire. "My uncle sees me as a child," he said after a while. "If I'd performed my rites last spring when Simo suggested it, Plaswa might have taken me along. He'd treat me as a man because I would be a man."

Kasko added wood to the fire. "We'll go in the spring," he offered. "Maybe Plaswa will take us both on the hunt next fall."

Ogistin drew his arms across his knees. "I'm not waiting for my rites until spring," he said. "I'll go as soon as our weeks of mourning are over." He lay down on his side, his face to the fire.

Kasko stared at his friend for a moment before he too lay down to sleep. The tamarack trees already glistened with golden needles. True winter seemed just a few weeks away. Ogistin was choosing to go off on his own during the harshest season. But Kasko didn't voice his concerns to his friend. It was, after all, Ogistin's decision.

2
Ogistin's Quest

O n an icy morning, a little more than three weeks later, Kasko came to bid his friend a good journey. Ogistin stood outside his family's cabin, shivering a little, as he waited for Kasko to reach him. Kasko held out a bundle of black wool. "Mother sends you this."

Ogistin thanked his friend and put the coat on over his leather tunic. Clothing made from the priest's cloth was highly prized. Kasko's mother had worked some red English ribbon in a line around the sleeves.

Ogistin knew the coat had been meant for Kasko.

"Your mother does fine work. Thank her for me, Kasko," Ogistin said.

Azô came out of the cabin carrying a few supplies. The boys said their good-byes, and Azô led Ogistin away from the village.

They walked for hours through the trees over the dusting of snow on the ground. When they stopped at last, Azô left a knife, ax, bow, and arrows at Ogistin's feet, along with two blankets, an empty water bag, and a leather medicine pouch. Ogistin would be alone—totally responsible for himself.

The boy sat against a tree until he could no longer hear the sounds of his father disappearing through the woods. He rubbed his feet, trying to ignore the cold that cut through his clothes.

When Ogistin felt that enough time had gone by, he stood and stretched, ready to begin preparing for the next four days. He'd been staring at a fallen tree that was wedged tightly between two smaller trees. It was high enough off the ground to hold cedar branches for a simple lean-to. He cut more than a dozen thick branches and leaned them against the log. Next he scraped some cedar bark and gathered dry pine needles to start a fire.

Ogistin took the fire-making kit from Simo's hunting bag. It took several tries before his stiff hands were able to coax a spark from the flint. As he worked, he thought of the day his brother had given him the bag.

"Take it, Ogistin," Simo had said, the night before the hunters had left. Ogistin took the moosehide pouch from his brother and stroked the quills their mother had designed into a cross. The pouch had been her gift to Simo when he had returned from his manhood rites. "You'll need it if you help Father hunt for the family while I'm gone," his brother said.

Ogistin had wanted to send his brother off on his first Long Hunt with a gift of equal value—something to show that he appreciated Simo's honor. "I have some things for you too that I've been saving for your trip." Ogistin had gone to his sleeping pallet and pulled out a small deerskin packet. Inside were dried tobacco leaves from the patch he'd tended all summer, two metal arrowheads he'd made from some broken knives, and six of his own lead bullets.

Simo had smiled his thanks and patted Ogistin's shoulder. "I'll use everything here, I know." He'd wrapped the items back in the deerskin and put the package with the gear he was taking with him.

Ogistin now wondered, as he worked, whether or not Simo had been able to use any of his gifts after all.

Ogistin added kindling and dried leaves to his fire, blowing lightly on the spark to give it life. He patiently added bigger pieces of wood. By dark, he was sitting inside his lean-to, wrapped in his blankets, watching the fire's glow. He was hungry and thirsty, but it didn't matter. For the first time since he'd learned of his brother's death, Ogistin felt as if things would soon be right.

He was freezing when he awoke and quickly revived his fire. It wasn't even dawn yet. Ogistin longed for some of his mother's good soup or a bit of meat. But this was the beginning of his fast. His father and uncle had told him that he must go without food for four days. Only then could his vision, his guardian spirit, be revealed to him.

He needed water. There was not enough snow on the ground to collect and melt. Not enough to pack alongside his shelter for warmth. But the woods were sloped and rocky, so it didn't take Ogistin long to follow the land and find a small stream. He filled his water bag and decided to try to make a container to heat the water. His father had left him a mixture of herbs to brew into tea.

Ogistin looked for a thick birch tree. The making of bark containers was usually done in the spring when the sap flowed and the bark was more pliable. But part of this test was to show that he was able to survive on his own.

He cut two circles around the trunk, nearly two feet

apart. He made a third cut down along the trunk to connect the circles. With his knife, he carefully pried a curved rectangle from the tree, warming his hands with his breath as he worked.

Ogistin sank the bark in the stream and held it down with two large rocks. He hoped the icy water would soften the bark. Then he dug in the frozen dirt with his knife around the trunk of a red spruce until he was able to pull out a long, thin, root. He put the spruce root in the stream to soften it along with the bark.

Ogistin collected as much wood, kindling, and dry bark as he could find. He built up his fire and stacked extra wood nearby. He added branches to his shelter. The work kept his mind focused away from his hunger.

After a few hours, he retrieved the birch bark and spruce root from the stream. Ogistin hoped they were soaked through.

He squatted close to the fire. The physical work of gathering wood and digging had kept him warm, but he quickly felt the cold now that he had stopped. Ogistin held the bark carefully above the flame, warming sections so they were softened by the heat but not burned.

He worked slowly. Sparks singed his hands and the front of his body grew too hot while his back felt too cold. But Ogistin forced himself to stay still and move his hands methodically. He was finally able to fold up part of each of the long sides of the rectangle to begin making a box. Next he folded up the short ends, creating triangle-shaped pockets at each corner.

Ogistin carefully pushed the pockets to the inside of the box. With the point of his knife, he made a few holes through each corner edge and tied the holes together with the spruce root. Then Ogistin scraped pitch from a nearby pine tree, warmed it until it was soft, and spread it on all the inside seams of the box to seal any leaks.

Adding water and the inner bark of the cedar tree, he set the box in the embers on the outermost edge of the campfire to brew tea. Then Ogistin opened the small medicine pouch and sprinkled some of the herbs it contained into the mixture.

While the tea brewed, Ogistin looked for another branch. He found a small, angled limb on the ground. His hands shook with cold as he scraped the bark off into his woodpile, smoothed the edges, and chipped away at the curve of the angled branch to form a spoon.

Ogistin dipped the spoon into the heated tea and slowly sipped the brew. His hands were shaking, and he was so hungry that drinking the tea was almost painful rather than soothing, but he forced himself to swallow a little.

He added wood to his fire and wrapped himself in a blanket. He stared into the flame and fell asleep, listening to the wind as tree branches clicked together, trying to imagine how his guardian spirit would come to him.

This time, when the predawn cold woke him, Ogistin was glad that he'd collected extra kindling and firewood. He was able to get a good flame again in a short time. As soon as he was warm enough, he left his shelter. It was important that he keep working in the cold and be ready if there came a time when, as his father had told him, he might not be able to move. The second day would be the hardest, Azô had warned him. He'd be very hungry, but still strong enough to hunt. He'd have to fight this urge and continue his fasting.

By midday, Ogistin was too tired to gather any more wood. The wind blew through his flimsy shelter as well as the layer of blankets and clothing in which he'd wrapped himself. Even the reheated tea gave him little comfort, but he drank more of the mixture and thought of home. His mother and Talaz would be cooking, he thought. Perhaps Mali and Agat would be helping Grandmother. And Azô would be hunting—alone—until Ogistin's return.

That thought convinced Ogistin he'd made the right decision. It was time to leave childhood behind. If the Pastoni murderers had kept him from being a man with Simo, he could at least become a man for Simo.

The tea made Ogistin sleepy. He dozed for several hours, beginning a pattern that would last for the next two days.

The boy stayed awake only long enough to collect more firewood and keep his fire burning. He was never warm now. His teeth chattered constantly, and his hands and feet felt numb when he moved too far from the fire. He wondered if he might freeze despite the fire. Could he keep the flames going as he grew weaker and the winds more bitter? He tried to remember the advice Azô and Plaswa had given him. He thought of things Simo had taught him. He prayed to Kdakinna, Grandmother Earth.

On the third day, Ogistin had gone beyond hunger. He began to dream, strange frightening dreams. He saw Simo's spirit, as handsome and strong as he was in life. Simo motioned to Ogistin to follow him into the forest. Ogistin begged his brother to stay, but Simo's face changed into a grotesque mask. It looked like an ancient tree, its knots creating angry eyes and a mouth. Simo's straight, black hair became yellow, and he wore a Pastoni hat. The face grew larger and larger, until it floated away from his body. It drifted up and disappeared beyond the trees.

Ogistin saw his family feasting on a great moose, but when he asked for a share of the meat, his father reminded him of his choice to leave. Ogistin saw his village in flames, the old people crying.

He drifted back in thought to his own fire. Only coals remained. Weakly, he fed the burning embers until he nursed a new flame. He struggled to stay awake to gather more wood to keep the fire going.

On the fourth day, Ogistin didn't leave his shelter. He could barely move from his blankets. He no longer felt very hot or cold.

In the dim light of the fireglow, Ogistin half opened his eyes. He squinted, for he thought he saw a large gray and brown cat crouched in the hut, holding a squirrel in his mouth. The cat's golden eyes held Ogistin's. For a long moment, the boy didn't move, thinking this was just another dream. The animal's tufted ears twitched, and then his short, black-tipped tail snapped to one side. Bezo! Ogistin thought.

Ogistin leaned up on an elbow. The sudden motion startled the lynx. The cat dropped the squirrel and crouched, ready to pounce.

Ogistin reached for a piece of firewood. Was the lynx sick? Ogistin could see no sign of it. But Bezo's strange behavior made him cautious. Ogistin waved the stick at the animal.

Bezo shrieked and pawed at the wood. Ogistin struggled to his knees, grabbed the stick with both hands and brought it down hard, missing the lynx. Bezo shrieked a high-pitched caterwaul and pounced at him. Ogistin swung the stick again and hit the wild cat full force in the muzzle. The lynx rolled with the blow, knocking down part of the lean-to. He scrambled up and jumped again, but Ogistin struck him in midjump. Bezo hung in the air for a moment, front claws and teeth caught in the wood.

Ogistin shook the stick, raising the branch up and down in heavy awkward movements. It was the third swing that did it, flipping Bezo on his back and forcing the branch down hard into the cat's mouth. Ogistin raised the stick again. But in two large, quiet leaps, the cat disappeared.

Ogistin knelt on the ground, breathing hard, staring at the lean-to entrance, ready to strike again. But the cat didn't return. When Ogistin finally relaxed, he looked down at the stick and saw something shining.

A tooth.

He pulled it from the wood. Yellow-white, large, and pointed—was this the sign Ogistin had been waiting for? His father had told him he'd know when his guardian spirit appeared. This lynx had come to Ogistin, right into his shelter, right up to his fire. Ogistin had never heard anyone tell such a tale. Bezo usually hid from people.

This would be Ogistin's secret, a tale he could share with no one.

Bezo, his uncle had told him, was a cunning hunter. "He'll sit patiently, high up in a tree," Plaswa said, "out of sight of his prey, and then he'll pounce without warning." Would this be Bezo's gift to him, Ogistin thought? To be a skillful hunter, able to hide from his prey like a lynx? He rubbed the tooth again, hoping it would be true.

Ogistin tried to remember what else his uncle had told him about Bezo. Why was it, he wondered, that hunters sometimes brought back the wild cat's soft gray pelts? And then he remembered: Bezo's great flaw was his inability to change. A hunter had but to find a lynx's den, and within days, he would learn the wild cat's route. No matter what, Bezo would return to his home.

What did this mean? Ogistin asked himself. Did it mean that he'd be so predictable that he'd be an easy target for his enemies?

No, it couldn't be that. Ogistin remembered what Grandmother sometimes said: habits could become weaknesses or strengths. Each person must choose. Bezo's habit also meant that the cat could always find his way home. He was able to sneak past a careless hunter to the shelter of his den.

The old ones called Bezo the secret-keeper. His golden eyes didn't betray the knowledge he kept in his soul. "Tell me your secrets, Bezo," Ogistin whispered. He put the tooth in Simo's bag. He would carry it with him always.

Ogistin thanked Kdakinna, Grandmother Earth,

for her protection. Then he made the sign of the cross on his head, heart, and shoulders to thank Gici Niwaskw, the Great Spirit, too. His quest was done.

He stoked the fire until warming flames were burning steadily. Ogistin found his knife, hidden under the crumpled pile of blankets. He skinned the squirrel Bezo had left, thanking the small animal for its life and nourishment.

Soon Ogistin had meat sizzling on a small spit. Enough meat to give him strength. In the morning, he'd walk back to his father's cabin. When he opened the door to greet his family, he knew he'd be greeting them as a man.

PART II

Five Years Later, April 1752
The Baker River

3
Trapper's Dilemma

ohn Stark cursed and flung the empty beaver trap so hard it smashed into a tree. He didn't care that he might've ruined the trap.

Of the dozen or so traps he'd set along the Baker River, only one held game. All the others he'd gathered that morning had been deliberately snapped.

John stepped out of the river and sat on a rock to rub some warmth back into his bare feet and give himself time to calm down. He walked over to the trap and checked it for damage. A couple of the teeth were bent. His brother, Will, would be angry at this carelessness, but John figured he could hammer out the dents when they got back home to Derryfield.

He put the broken trap with the others he'd gathered and collected his boots and musket. He walked along the riverbank, avoiding shady spots that still held thick patches of April snow. Even here, at the foot of the White Hills, winter was leaving. Will was right—it was time to head home. Their trapping partners, Amos Eastman and David Stinson, had talked of staying a bit longer, but they'd all agreed it would soon be too warm for good pelts, for the animals would be shedding their winter fur.

John reached the next trap. It, too, had been snapped. A long, thick stick protruded from the river. He pulled at it, bringing his trap with it.

When he'd found the first one, John had thought David had been playing a prank. He and David had been keeping up a friendly running argument about which of them was the better trapper. They'd planned to settle the bet after they collected this last round of furs.

All the men had managed to get a good lot of pelts during the weeks they'd been trapping near the Pemi and Baker rivers, and they had agreed to share the profits. David thought the furs were worth at least five hundred pounds sterling. He might undo one or two of John's traps in order to sway the odds in his favor, but he would never have gone this far to win the bet. Such high jinks would have cost all four of them.

John forced himself to remain calm. He carefully opened the trap and removed the branch. Whoever was doing this knew exactly where his traps had been set. The group had not seen another trapper in these parts in all the time they'd been here. That left only one other possibility, and John was not sure he wanted to consider it—Indians. His ma had warned him.

"You'll be too far from any settlement, trapping that far north," she had said. "There've been savages all over those parts. I'll not have my boys in danger!"

But John and Will's pa had taken their side. "Eleanor, your boys are *men!* Twenty-four and twenty-eight—old enough for soldiering, old enough to care for themselves!"

John and Will hadn't been worried. The last war with the French and their Indian allies had ended four years earlier. There were still a few skirmishes between the English colonists and the Indians, but nothing they worried about too much.

Besides, John reminded himself as he pushed on to the last of the traps, he had Will, David, and Amos. Together they'd be able to handle any problems.

He put his bundle down on the riverbank. The

water was calmer here, and clear. He could see the trap underwater, with an oak branch caught between its metal teeth. He stood a moment, staring at it, frustrated. There was nothing to do but get that one too. He let out a breath and waded into the icy water, pulling the trap out of the water and bringing it back to shore. He began to remove the stick but stopped.

Something had changed. The Baker River, swollen by the spring thaw, thundered as loudly as before. But the woods were too quiet. The hair on the back of John's neck prickled. He turned around quickly and was blinded by the sun. He shaded his eyes to help him focus.

John blinked and tried to look beyond the sandy bank into the forest. When his vision cleared, he realized that he was not looking at trees at all. He was looking at men.

4
Ogistin's First Prisoner

Ogistin had a clear shot of the Pastoni standing at the edge of the river. He could have killed him, but Plaswa stopped him.

"There are others, Ogistin," he whispered. "They're worth more to us alive."

Toma nodded. "The French pay well for them."

"I'll avenge my brother's death." Ogistin spoke quietly, the rifle butt against his shoulder.

Plaswa looked down into his nephew's eyes. "There

are many forms of revenge. The Pastoni took your brother from all of us."

Ogistin looked from Plaswa to Toma to Kasko and some of the others. He respected all of these men, his uncle most of all. He turned back to Plaswa and let the calm in the older man's dark eyes soothe his own anger.

The hunters had been working their way home when they'd found the Pastoni traps. It had been easy to snap the traps and wait for the white men to return.

A single trapper had come down the river. When Plaswa gave the signal, all ten Abenaki hunters had stepped out of the shadows, just as the Pastoni turned and looked toward them. He could not reach his weapon and was easily captured. This was the first time Ogistin and Kasko had been along when a Pastoni prisoner had been taken. Ogistin was so excited he forgot his place and stood behind the prisoner, poking his gun into the white man's back.

"Ogistin," Plaswa commanded, "collect the Pastoni's traps and gun."

Ogistin was furious with himself. As one of the youngest in the group, he should have waited for Plaswa's orders. He'd let the memory of Simo's death get in the way.

Kasko, now nearly as tall as his father, Lobal, looked at Ogistin. He understood what his friend was feeling but didn't let his sympathy show. He would not embarrass Ogistin further.

Lobal took Ogistin's place behind the Pastoni, while Toma and Kasko knelt to help Ogistin gather the musket, traps, and boots.

"Most of the Pastoni traps are in good shape," Toma said. "We can use them ourselves to trap more game."

Ogistin nodded. "More furs to trade and a Pastoni to sell to the French." He glared at the prisoner, who was standing silently, his back arched against Lobal's gun. The Pastoni was tall, slim, and strongly built. His hair was nearly as dark as the Abenakis' and tied in a short tail. He wore the woolen breeches and jacket favored by the English.

Plaswa spoke the prisoner's language. He'd learned the English tongue while fur trading in Albany. The prisoner pointed away from the river.

"Give the Pastoni his boots," Plaswa told Kasko. "He says his friends are west of here."

"What if he lies?" one of the others asked.

"I told him his friends would live if he told the truth," Plaswa answered. "We can sell all of them."

The prisoner put on his boots and walked slowly ahead of Lobal. The hunters searched the ground for footprints and scanned the woods for movement.

"The Pastoni are cowards and thieves," Toma whispered. "They measure land and tell us to hunt in the north." Toma was smaller than Ogistin and wiry. His movements were as quick as his temper.

"This was the home of my ancestors, the Pennacook and the Pemigewassett," Toma went on, waving his arm in a great circle. "It's *our* right to hunt in these parts. My grandfather was here trapping beaver when more than thirty whites ambushed them."

"Your grandfather lived?" Ogistin asked.

"Yes, he and some of the others returned to the village to protect the women and children, and warn the others. But the Pastoni killed the ones who stayed behind. My grandfather said they never even greeted the Chief of the Hunting Party or tried to speak to him. They fired as soon as they saw the hunters."

Toma scowled. "The next day, my grandfather and the other men led their families to St. Francis."

Sazal, walking ahead of them, had heard what Toma said. "The Pastoni Governor knows these woods are still our home," Sazal told Ogistin. "I was with the Chief Speaker when he spoke to the Governor's men. Atecouando told them of our people's rights."

"Yes," Toma answered, "but the Governor didn't tell *his* people. They still try to take furs that should be ours. We'll teach these Pastoni savages the truth."

"We'll take them as easily as they killed Simo and the others, won't we, Kasko?" Ogistin said, turning to his friend.

Kasko didn't reply. Over the years, Ogistin thought, his friend had become more like his quiet father, Lobal, speaking only after he'd given thought to his words. Instead of answering, Kasko turned to look at the prisoner. Ogistin followed his friend's stare. The white man walked quietly and showed no emotion.

"I wish I could have been with you, Toma," Ogistin said, "when Simo was killed."

"You're here today," Toma said. "It's never too late for revenge."

The sun beat down more strongly as the hunting party continued their search. They walked for a while without finding any sign of the other Pastoni. Had the prisoner lied to protect his friends?

Ogistin had met French and Pastoni traders in his village. They were men who lived and hunted alone. None of them would risk his life to save someone else's skin.

Musket shot sounded in the distance. The prisoner looked back toward the sound. Plaswa shouted: "The Pastoni's friends are behind us! Come!"

There was a second blast. Plaswa hit the Pastoni hard in the back with the butt of his gun.

"Bring him!" Plaswa shouted to Lobal. "He'll pay for his lies later."

5
Captured!

ohn heard the Abenaki leader shout, then pain shot through his back, and his breath left his body in one huge blast. A hunter grabbed him and dragged him along.

John swore silently. He'd tried to lead his captors far enough away so Will and the others could escape. He hadn't counted on them firing signal shots. He couldn't warn them now. They'd wait, and fire again, hoping for his return signal.

John's captors moved quickly through the forest.

The guard poked him frequently in the back, forcing him to keep up. John could think of no way to slow the Indians' progress.

Another shot. They were very near. The Indians slowed their pace, and hid behind trees and large rocks. John's guard kept him several feet behind the rest of the group.

The leader faced John again. "Your friends are in the clearing ahead. Call to them and tell them to come to you."

John walked to the clearing. The Indians could have killed him before, John thought. There had to be a reason they wanted him alive. He could see the waters of the Baker joining the Pemigewassett River just a few hundred feet away. He saw Will and David tying bundles of pelts. Amos was piling traps. John could feel ten muskets pointing at his back.

"John!" Amos shouted when he caught sight of him. "We'd just about given up on you." Amos smiled at John, bent down, grabbed a huge bundle of pelts, and hitched them to his back.

"Where'd you leave your gear, Johnny? We're about ready to leave." Amos grunted, and bent again, dropping his fur cap as he tried to shift the pack to a more comfortable position.

John kept his face serious and walked steadily toward the group. He stared at Will, hoping to signal his brother without words.

"Where're the traps, Johnny?" Will asked, puzzled. Then his face changed, and he picked up his musket, slowly.

John had no idea what was going on behind him. He tried to make his voice sound as if he were simply greeting his friends. "Get out, Will."

There was a rush from behind. To his left, he saw Amos panic and try to run with the load of pelts on his back. Ahead of him, David and Will were running, running toward the Pemi.

Muskets were fired from shore. The sulfur smell filled John's nostrils.

"Ruuunn, Will!" John screamed as he grabbed one of the Indian guns. Someone knocked him to the ground and kicked him.

Will shot his musket, injuring one of the Abenaki. He turned and ran into the Pemi, creating huge splashes as he went. Two of the hunters chased him, but he stayed just ahead of them.

John tried to grab one of the Indian's legs, but another man hit John on the back of the head with something hard. John's eyes clouded, but before the sky and river and trees became gray and then disappeared, he saw David jumping into the Pemi. And he thought he saw Will—running on the other side.

6
Ogistin's Settlement

ne Pastoni had escaped, but the red-haired one was being swept downstream, out of range. Ogistin ran along the shore, aimed, and pulled the trigger, but there was no sound. His flint was wet.

Before he could react, he heard an explosion of gunfire behind him. He turned to see Toma lowering his gun. When Ogistin looked back at the river, the red-haired one was disappearing underwater. Ogistin threw his musket down and jumped into the freezing river. The Pastoni was tall and weighted down by his wet clothing, but Ogistin managed to pull him toward shore. Kasko and Toma ran out to help him drag the body ashore.

The Pastoni's hair clung to his head, and blood began to seep through a hole in the man's coat. The three hunters stood staring for only a moment; then Toma took charge. He pulled a powder horn from around the dead man's neck. "Here, Ogistin, take this. This Pastoni should've been yours." He threw the horn to Ogistin and searched through the dead man's clothes for other bounty.

"My flint was wet," Ogistin said, catching the horn and pulling the brass cap off the end of it. He poured a bit of powder into his hand. "The powder's still dry." He shoved the cap back on and examined the powder horn more closely. It was polished smooth, almost shiny. The ends were tied by pieces of leather strapping. He put the loop over his shoulder.

Kasko had gone upriver and returned with Ogistin's gun. "The others are heading north," he said, handing Ogistin the musket.

"Wait," Toma answered. He took out his knife and looked at Ogistin. "We can't let this one haunt us."

Ogistin pushed the gun back into Kasko's hand and let the powder horn slide to the ground.

"Then let me do it," he said. "The Pastoni have stalked my dreams long enough."

He took the long skinning knife from the sheath that hung around his neck, wound a fistful of the reddish strands in his left hand and pulled the man's head back. In a few awkward jerks, it was done. He let the river rinse the Pastoni blood from his knife and stuffed the scalp into Simo's hunting bag.

"Now *you* control *his* soul," Toma hissed. He finished rifling through the dead man's clothes. "Here's a knife and some bullets. Leave the rest."

Ogistin grabbed the powder horn, Kasko gathered up the muskets, and they took off after Toma.

They followed the Pemigewassett River north, deep into the White Hills. Lobal dragged the first prisoner while the second one, the bearded one, walked behind them, guarded by Kôgôwés. Some of the other men from St. Francis, like Sazal, were farther ahead, lugging their furs and the piles of furs the white hunters had taken. Paslid struggled to keep up despite his bleeding leg. Kasko handed the muskets to Ogistin and helped Paslid along.

Plaswa called a halt in the early evening, and they prepared camp on the riverbank. Lobal left both the prisoners with Kôgôwés while he went off with two others to find something to eat. Sazal prepared the campfires. As the youngest hunters, Ogistin and

Kasko had the job of getting the water. In St. Francis, such work was done by children, but the young men didn't complain. They were here to learn. If they did well, they'd be invited to join the older men again. Someday, younger boys would tote the camp water.

They took water carriers from each man. The carriers were hollowed-out gourds or pouches made from deer or moose stomachs. The boys carefully placed the containers in the water so as not to stir up any grit from the river bottom. The men would be angry to have muddy water to drink.

When Ogistin was finished, he took a small wooden cup that hung from his waist cinch, helped himself to a drink, then passed the cup to Kasko.

"What was it like?" Kasko asked. This was the first time one of them had been in battle, and the first time either of them had taken a scalp. Ogistin thought a while before answering. "It doesn't make up for Simo, or the grandchildren my mother might have had, but it helps. For all I know, that Pastoni might have been there when my brother was killed, might have even killed him. Maybe this one has a family who'll mourn him like we still mourn Simo."

7
The Captives' Fate

ohn thought he was opening his eyes, but everything was still black. As he became able to focus, he realized he was looking up into the night sky. There was no moon, and the tiny stars were barely visible.

John couldn't move. He was cold, wet, and in pain. Why did he feel so bad? He closed his eyes again, and remembered: musket fire, Will running.

"Johnny?" a voice whispered. "Johnny, wake up."

John forced his eyes open and tried to raise his

head. Everything hurt at once, and his mouth felt unbelievably dry. "Amos?" He wasn't sure he had managed to say the word out loud.

"I'm right here, behind you. Don't move."

"Did...Will...make...it?"

"I think so. He wasn't hit, and they didn't go after him. They shot David, I think."

"Where are we?" John turned his head slightly. His eyes cleared, and he could see sparks from a campfire rising into the sky like orange starlight. John tried to lick his lips. It was so hard to talk.

"We've been heading north," Amos answered. The English-speaking leader suddenly loomed above John. "Get up, Pastoni." He pulled on John's arms. John took in a sharp breath, gritted his teeth in pain, and stood up. He closed his eyes again to stop the spinning that came from the sudden movement. Then he and Amos were pushed toward the fire.

Three rabbit carcasses were cooking on a spit. He and Amos were told to sit and were each given water to drink. Several of the hunters were gathered near the fire, talking quietly. Most of the men seemed his age or a bit older. One hunter was so tall and large that he almost seemed to be a giant. There were also two boys—nearly men. One was tall, thin, and long legged, the other shorter but more muscular.

The Indians wore buckskin leggings. Some of them topped these with leather tunics; others wore French or English style jackets. They all wore their hair long and loose. A few had knotted one or two large gray or black feathers in their hair. The feathers hung over one ear.

John was surprised when he and Amos were given shares of the rabbit meat equal to those of their captors. Three rabbits didn't provide much food for twelve men, but the smell of food turned John's stomach. He offered his share to Amos.

"You should eat, John. Keep your strength up."

John shook his head. "I'll probably feel more like eating tomorrow."

The Abenaki leader crouched near Amos and John. The others in the group turned to watch. "I am Plaswa," he said simply.

"I'm Amos Eastman, and this is John Stark." Amos's words were clipped and a bit too loud. "What do you want with us?"

Plaswa's face was expressionless. His voice was calm, like a parent explaining a fact to a child. "I do not want you. *You* came to this land. *You* tried to take furs that belong to us."

"What're you talking about?" Amos was yelling. "My partners and I trapped those furs ourselves. We took nothing from you Indians."

"There've been no Indian settlements here for nearly forty years," John added, his voice a croaky whisper. "This land belongs to the Crown now."

"You Pastoni and your illnesses drove away the People, who once lived here. But that does not make the land yours. Do you own the river once you have removed the fish? Can the sky be yours because you have killed the geese? Our families have hunted here for many generations. Pastoni do not belong here."

Plaswa motioned to the bundles of furs that were stacked nearby. "We will keep the pelts, Amos Eastman. And you are our prisoners. We did not come here to find Pastoni. We came to hunt for our village. Tomorrow we will continue our hunt. When we are finished, we will bring you to St. Francis."

Amos turned to John. St. Francis! The Abenaki village was in the French-held territory of Quebec, more than a hundred miles north. John could see the panic in Amos's eyes, but the news gave him some hope. If Plaswa was telling them the truth, he was also telling them that he planned to keep them alive for now. Maybe Will would come back for them, or they'd be able to escape. Surely Amos could see it too. But his friend's face was somber, his head hung in despair. Plaswa turned to one of the young hunters—the shorter one—and spoke to him.

The boy didn't argue, but his face showed slight annoyance. He took a wooden drinking cup from his belt, filled it with water, and swished the bowl of the cup over the campfire flame.

John watched his movements. Despite his obvious

strength, the boy's arms stuck out from his leather tunic as if he were not quite finished growing into his body. The young man took a few dry leaves from a small brown pouch and swirled them around the warm water with a stick. He brought the mixture to John.

"Drink, John Stark," Plaswa said. "It will help you heal."

John took a sip. The drink was warmer than he expected and burned his tongue. The mixture smelled odd but not unpleasant. John could detect wintergreen, a remedy his ma often used. He drank slowly, feeling his stomach settle.

"I have told my nephew to make more if you ask," Plaswa said. "He is called Ogistin. He does not speak your language, but if you say his name, he will know what you want." The young Abenaki crouched on his haunches facing John and Amos.

Plaswa walked away to join some of the other men.

"Look, Johnny," Amos said, keeping his eyes on the boy. "He's got David's powder horn."

"I saw it too," John said.

The boy seemed to wait until Plaswa was busy with other matters. Then Ogistin opened the quilled pouch that hung from the middle of his belt, pulled something out, and held it in his hands.

In the dark, with only the light of a campfire throwing shadows around them, John wasn't sure, at first, what Ogistin held. But when John recognized the reddish tinge in the lock of hair, his stomach lurched. He glared at Ogistin. Ogistin returned the stare. John couldn't read the meaning in the boy's dark eyes.

8
A Plan
and a Vision

gistin put the scalp back into Simo's hunting bag, got up, and left the prisoners. He found Kasko checking the Pastoni traps. Ogistin sat near his friend and chuckled soflty. "My uncle was right. There are many forms of revenge."

"What do you mean?" Kasko asked.

Ogistin took one of the traps and checked it for dents or broken parts. He explained about the Pastoni scalp while he worked. "You should've seen their faces," Ogistin said. "The bearded one looked sick, and the other one wanted to choke me, I think."

"Why do you bother so much with those two?" Kasko asked. "These Pastoni mean nothing to us. Only the French will be interested in them—for how much work they can get out of them." He put down the trap and reached for another.

Ogistin jerked Kasko's arm aside and glared at him. "Pastoni killed my brother and Pastoni—no matter who they are—will pay."

Kasko pulled his arm away and frowned at Ogistin. "You're acting like a cornered animal, Ogistin. They're the prisoners after all."

"You're wrong, Kasko," Ogistin said. "Why can't you see my side of it? These Pastoni deserve to be punished. A friend would be offering to help, not sitting by doing nothing."

Kasko looked up patiently. "And what is it, exactly, you want me to do?"

Ogistin grinned. "I knew I could depend on you."

"Simo was a brother to me too."

"Then help me make them see how foolish they were when they tried to take from the Abenaki."

Kasko looked away as if to consider what Ogistin was saying. "Plaswa will never let us hurt them. The French will pay nothing for dead Pastoni. The whites aren't at war. Even an English scalp is worth little now."

"That's not my plan."

Kasko handed Ogistin another trap. "We're here to hunt, Ogistin. We've both worked hard to get Plaswa to notice us and invite us along. Why waste your time with the Pastoni? Wouldn't it be better to show that we're good hunters and worth taking along again? You'll get your revenge for Simo soon enough. Be patient." Kasko stood up and went to lie by the fire.

Ogistin slammed down the trap and walked a short distance away. He sat alone, leaning against a large oak tree. If Kasko wouldn't help him, he thought, then he'd handle the Pastoni himself.

Ogistin raised his shoulders to stretch them. He was tired after the long day. So much had happened in such a short time. He leaned his head back and stared at the starlight through the oak tree's branches.

Light from the campfires made moving shadows in the tree. Ogistin watched the dancing shadows turn gray, then black, then gray again. He was angry at Kasko, but more angry at himself. He simply hadn't been convincing enough. Kasko just didn't understand, that's all. He'd explain it all again in the morning.

Ogistin took a long slow breath. His body relaxed, and he crossed his arms over his chest and stretched out his legs. The shadows began to take shape, and he imagined the shapes were animals and birds. He pictured the owl, Kokokhas, sitting on a high branch, digging her sharp talons into the tree limb. Huge, round eyes pierced the darkness.

Then Azeban appeared in the firelight, scrambling from his hole in the tree. The raccoon ignored Kokokhas as he scrounged for food. His plump body moved noiselessly, sniffing at this and poking at that.

The campfire popped, sending a splash of orange embers into the air. Two large, round sparks remained suspended in the branches. Their glow outlined a shape resting on one of the lower limbs, just above Ogistin's head. The circles changed from orange to gold. The shape became ghostlike, gray, soft.

Bezo stared silently at Ogistin. The cat's ears did not move, his tail twitched only slightly. Ogistin stared back, unafraid, patient.

Ogistin could see Bezo's face clearly. There was a small stain of blood on the cat's muzzle. Bezo had had a successful hunt. The lynx lifted a moistened paw and rubbed it over the stain until it disappeared.

Ogistin's breathing slowed. He was alone with the lynx. Kokokhas had flown silently away. Azeban was nowhere in sight. The campfire had burned so low that he couldn't see the other men. Only Bezo was visible in the ember glow.

The great cat finished cleaning its fur. No sign of the hunt remained on the lynx. He crouched on his branch gazing out into the blackness, his golden eyes slightly hooded.

"Ah, Bezo," Ogistin murmured. "You captured your prey because it was weaker than you. I captured my prey today too. But I tried to strike too soon. I forgot to be patient like you, Great Cat." Ogistin vowed he would not let his impatience get in the way again.

Bezo turned his face away from Ogistin, not interested in the boy's words. The animal stood and walked along the tree limb. The branch began to sway with the weight of the cat. Then the lynx fixed his eyes on Ogistin's once more. Ogistin watched the cat's front legs begin to lower. The hind legs gave a mighty push. Bezo was sailing, down...down... down...

Ogistin grunted. The pain on his chest was sharp. He jumped up, putting his hand on his knife. He couldn't see the lynx anywhere.

"What is it?" Kasko asked, now also alert.

"Did you see it?" Ogistin whispered.

"See what?" Kasko stood up and looked around.

No one moved. Even the prisoners lay quiet, their backs to the fire. Ogistin searched the forest, but saw no movement. The two young men stood perfectly still, watching and waiting. The only sounds were the soft cracklings of the campfires and the quiet breathing of sleeping men.

"You were dreaming," Kasko said finally as he lay back down.

"No, I couldn't have been. I was awake imagining animal shapes in..." Ogistin stopped. His explanation sounded ridiculous even to himself. He must have been asleep after all. He lay down and thought about Bezo, and the dream. His grandmother would have told him to listen to the message in his dream. He wasn't sure why he had dreamed about Bezo, but he knew the dream had seemed so real that he could still feel the pain on his chest where the lynx had landed.

Then Ogistin noticed his wooden drinking cup at his feet and understood what had caused the pain.

9

On to
St. Francis

Pitching the water cup at Ogistin had been a careless act. But the sight of David's scalp had angered John beyond logical thought.

At least Amos didn't know what John had done. John had waited, listening to Amos's soft snores, before he threw the cup. He'd had a moment of satisfaction when he heard Ogistin's surprised grunt. John had lain, his back to the fire, waiting for Ogistin's next move.

He hurt with the strain of lying perfectly still. He was ready to fight Ogistin—and all the others if he had to. John calculated the odds in his head. He wasn't tied, but the Abenaki had weapons. Ogistin might try to attack him in his sleep. He'd surprise the boy and pretend to sleep. John closed his eyes and breathed slowly.

In. Out.

In...Out.

In....Out....

John thought only minutes had passed when he suddenly felt himself being shaken. He opened his eyes with a start and saw that it was already dawn. The largest Indian in the hunting party—the one they called Lobal—had John by the front of his jacket. Lobal shook John as if to satisfy himself that John was truly awake, then did the same with Amos. "What!" Amos yelled. Lobal let Amos drop and leaned against a tree to watch the prisoners, his musket loosely draped across his arms.

There were still traces of stars in the gray-blue sky. John had been asleep for hours. Ogistin hadn't come after him.

The Abenaki hunters were moving quickly, gathering supplies. John nudged Amos and gestured toward the group. "They're breaking camp," he whispered.

Each Abenaki took a load of furs, traps, or dried

meat to carry. Amos was handed his own bundle of pelts. John received a large pack to haul as well. Only one man, the one Will had shot in the leg, wasn't given anything to carry except his musket and a tall walking stick. His thigh was wrapped with a makeshift bandage of leather strips.

"I'd say they've been at this for a while," Amos said, looking at the great piles of skins the Indians were carrying.

John nodded. "The traders in Albany claim the French Indians get the best skins on their Long Hunts. Maybe that's what we've had the misfortune of stumbling upon, Amos."

"I mean this to be the last of *my* misfortunes," Amos answered as he tied his bundle to his back. "I don't intend to end up like David."

John lowered his voice. He wasn't sure if, like Plaswa, some of the other hunters might understand English. "Are you saying you wouldn't try to escape?"

"I'm saying I don't know," Amos whispered back. "I'm saying let's be careful."

Before Amos could go on, Lobal poked him in the shoulder with his gun and signaled Amos to follow the rest of the hunting party. A few led the way. Others spread out as scouts, but the one they called Ogistin hung back with Lobal to trail John and Amos.

The Abenaki hunters kept a swift pace, following

deer paths north into the White Hills. Pine trees kept the woods dark, and the spring mountain air was cold enough that some snow remained. The cool air did little to refresh John and Amos. They were soon thirsty and hot.

John's anger hadn't cooled either. He kept remembering the sight of David's scalp lying in Ogistin's hand.

"Are you all right, Johnny?" Amos asked after they'd been walking for some time. John had walked most of the stiffness out of his body, but the pack he carried bounced against his back, reminding him of the beating he'd received. "I could do with some water," was all he said in reply.

"Ow!" Amos cried out, reaching for his head. "Something hit me."

John turned to look at Amos and saw Ogistin watching him. There was a small trickle of blood behind Amos's ear.

The boy poked his gun in Amos's back to force him to keep walking. Things were quiet for only a short time before John, too, felt something hit the back of his head. He jerked in surprise, but didn't look back at Ogistin.

Amos saw what happened. "It's the boy, isn't it?" he whispered. "Do you suppose he intends to keep at us all day?"

"I'd wager he's going to try."

John deliberately ran outside the deer path the others were following. Ogistin jumped in front of Amos and chased John into the brush. John waited until Ogistin was nearly on him and let a long branch snap back into the boy's face. Ogistin yelped in pain, and John laughed. Ogistin hit John in the chest with the butt of his musket knocking him to the ground.

In seconds, two of the other hunters stood by Ogistin, forming a circle around John. Plaswa rushed up and questioned Ogistin.

"It's foolish to try and escape, John Stark," Plaswa said in a commanding voice.

"I was just looking for water," John said. "The day's getting warm."

"We will stop soon enough." Plaswa handed his water bag to John. Lobal did the same for Amos. As the prisoners drank, Plaswa sent the boy and one of the other men to the front of the line. He remained behind with Lobal. "It would be best," he said as he took the water bag back, "if you did not try to look for streams, Pastoni."

Plaswa held his gun on John, and Lobal dragged him up by one arm. The Chief of the Hunt glared at John for an instant, then turned to take his place toward the front of the line. Lobal motioned for Amos to join John, and the march began again.

They made camp near a brook. John unloaded his heavy pack and let himself drop to the ground. Amos did the same. He wasted no time telling John what he thought. "Stop being a fool, Johnny!" he said.

John frowned. "What do you want me to do, Amos? Let some stupid boy get the better of me?"

"We're the prisoners here," Amos said. "That stupid boy as you call him is just as savage as the rest of 'em. He could slice your scalp off in your sleep if he got the notion."

"Like David's, you mean? We owe it to David to fight back." John tried to keep his voice level.

Amos rolled his eyes. "David's dead. But we're alive, and I intend to stay that way."

"I do too, Amos. But we can't give in to them. What if Will comes after us in a few days?"

"How far do you think he's gotten?" Amos asked.

"Not far. Even if Will kept up a good pace, it'd take him a few days to reach Rumford," John said.

"And *if* he can get anyone to come after us, it'll take a few days more," Amos said. "Whether your brother makes it back to Derryfield, it's not likely anyone'll risk another war with the Indians to come after the two of us! Other people have their own survival to consider. The Abenaki didn't attack our town. And it's nearly planting time. Who's going to risk losing a whole crop to come after two men?"

"Then we'll have to fight them ourselves, Amos. We won't let them take us to St. Francis."

Amos grabbed John's jacket and spoke into his

face: "Johnny, my father lived near Dunstable town when two of their men were taken. They didn't come back for *two years!* Two long years they were forced to work for the French. But at least they came back. The fools that went after them are all lying in a single grave."

John scoffed. "We've all heard your pa tell that tale a hundred times."

"Yes, but he had his point." Amos let go of John's jacket. "Sometimes people need to stand together, but sometimes it's best to stand alone. The Indians are in control here. The sooner you keep that in mind, the better off we'll both be."

Amos walked a short distance away and turned his back on John.

John found a clear spot on the ground. He pulled down some hemlock branches to lie on. The nights were cold, and the prospect of lying on damp ground didn't appeal to him. He stretched out on his evergreen nest and thought about the argument he'd had with his friend.

Amos was wrong. And he was going to prove it. No Indian was going to better John Stark. And this one was just a boy. He wouldn't let Ogistin win.

John thought about the great chance he'd taken when he'd flung the cup at Ogistin. The Abenaki could have punished him, but hadn't. Had the boy kept the incident to himself? It seemed that way.

Ogistin had simply pelted a few stones. Maybe Plaswa wouldn't allow him to do more. Or maybe Ogistin was just waiting.

During the next few days, as they kept on marching north, the conflict continued. Ogistin began to ignore Amos and focus on John, taking every opportunity to torment him.

John couldn't prove that the dirt he found in his food had been put there by Ogistin. He couldn't say for sure that it was Ogistin who tripped him or spit at him. But whenever these things happened, the boy was nearby, watching. John tried to fight Ogistin in his own way, without forgetting that he was a prisoner. He walked as slowly as he dared, forcing the others to wait for him. He loosened the knots that held his pack of pelts so that it fell apart when he hitched the bundle to his back. The hunters were delayed even more as they waited for John to retie the skins.

No one commented about anything that John or Ogistin did. Amos would roll his eyes in disgust, but Plaswa appeared not to notice John and Ogistin searching for ways to aggravate each other.

The hunters stopped each evening to rest and eat. After a few days, they made a more permanent camp

where they stayed more than a week, hunting, preparing furs, drying the meat. Then the pattern repeated itself: three or four days of walking and resting followed by a longer hunting camp.

The farther north they went, John knew, the less possible escape became.

One night, Plaswa made Amos and John sit with him by the fire. Ogistin and his friend sat a distance away, talking softly and sharpening their knives. Other men played some sort of gambling game with marked sticks.

"How much longer until we get to St. Francis?" Amos asked the leader.

"Perhaps two or three weeks," Plaswa replied.

John decided to try his luck. "Plaswa," he said, "you have more than you expected to get. You don't need two prisoners. This is a time of peace between the English and the Abenaki."

Plaswa looked into the fire before he replied. When he began to speak, his voice took on the rhythm of a storyteller: "When the first whites came from across the great ocean, they saw only riches. They came to fish and hunt for furs. They took the tallest trees for their ships and the choicest strips of land for their homes and farms. The rest they wasted.

"The Wabanaki were a great nation in those days. The Pennacook and Pawtucket and others lived to the south. The Kennebec, Penobscot and Passamaquoddy lived to the east. They were strong, skilled hunters and fishermen.

"These ancestors took pity on the strangers. In friendship, they taught them how to make snowshoes and canoes, how to grow corn and cook meat in sweet, boiled sap.

"The whites gave us tools made of metal, and guns that could kill more quickly than our weapons. But they brought something else: sickness. Thousands died. Entire families were killed by invisible enemies. The great peoples were weakened. We lost our old people: our wisdom and our stories. Children lost mothers, and mothers lost children. The strong, skilled hunters and warriors died.

"The whites wrote words on paper that said the whites now owned the land. But because our people did not read the words the whites wrote or understand the ways of the white God, the whites called our people ignorant. Yet few whites tried to understand the symbols we used, or tried to learn about the ways of Kdakinna, Grandmother Earth. We know well that no one can own Kdakinna. The trees, the animals, even the stones have their own spirits. Each give of themselves so the People can live.

"Then the many different whites began to fight

among themselves. The French lived among us peacefully, and when they asked for our help, we gave it. But the Pastoni have never been willing to live among us. Whether in war or peace, they have called us savages and treated us like dogs. They have killed our women and children to get us out of the way and make our numbers less.

"Our people who survived took their families north to live among the French. The Pennacook, the Sokoki, the Abenaki, and others became one family. We share our languages and our skills. Even now, people are leaving their homes to come to St. Francis. They know they will be safe there.

"You, John Stark, say this is not war, but you came here to take furs. You do not respect us or our ways, and yet you want us to respect you. It is the Pastoni, not the Abenaki, who measure land. But then you do not even honor the measurements and agreements you have made with us. Our Chief Speaker, Atecouando, has told your Governor that we will defend what is ours."

"It may have been Abenaki land once, Plaswa," John said, "but it belongs to the Crown now. The Crown claimed the land up to the great Winnepesoga Lake long ago." After Plaswa's words, John's explanation sounded weak even to himself.

"The Governor also agreed, long ago, to return the hunting rights to the Abenaki," Plaswa answered. "We took this as a gesture of peace."

John shrugged. "Maybe what you say is true, Plaswa. But don't you agree that you don't need us? You have our furs. What good are prisoners—unless it's to amuse Ogistin?"

Plaswa let out an impatient breath. "You think I do not see the things you do to my nephew. And Ogistin, because he is young and sees with young eyes, does not know that I watch him too. He has much anger because the Pastoni killed Simo, his brother. Ogistin still uses his anger like a child rather than like a man. But as for you, John Stark and Amos Eastman, you have no regard for us. You say that this is not war. But I tell you, it cannot be called peace. It has never been peace."

Plaswa called to Ogistin. The boy glanced at his friend and then came to sit a respectful distance from his uncle. The conversation between the leader and the young hunter was brief. John didn't understand what was being said, but he thought he heard his name. By the time Plaswa was finished, Ogistin's expression had hardened.

Then Plaswa turned to John and explained, "I have told my nephew that you will answer to him. You will do the work he assigns. You will hunt with him. I have also told him that I expect to arrive in St. Francis with *two* prisoners. He is now responsible for your life."

10
Enemy Trappers

gistin was furious with his uncle's decision. "We tire of the pranks you insist on playing," Plaswa had said. "We're here to work. Your mind hasn't been on the work we need to do. We should have left you in St. Francis." His uncle hadn't said "to work in the garden with the women and children," but Ogistin knew what he meant—and was humiliated.

"Since you seem to think only of John Stark and can't think of the furs that must be trapped so our village can trade," Plaswa continued, "then you may have John Stark, but remember this—he's as important to our village as the pelts. I expect him to arrive in St. Francis in good health."

So Plaswa had known what he'd been up to all along. That didn't mean Ogistin had to stop. The prisoner only had to arrive in St. Francis in good health. They were weeks away from home.

A snow squall came up during the night, blanketing the ground with a few inches of fresh snow. Toma and some of the other men tracked a young buck they planned to chase down, so Toma sent one of his group back to camp to get Kasko and some of the others. Although Ogistin was a good runner, he was not invited to go.

"John Stark can stay with his friend," Ogistin told his uncle. "Lobal can guard them both."

"I'm sure Toma would have liked your help," Plaswa answered. "But you made your choice about John Stark. You'll set beaver traps instead."

"But it's nearly spring, Plaswa. Surely we're finished with trapping. The young will be born soon."

"There are a few days before the full moon. We have time left. You know these things, Ogistin." Plaswa's voice was firm.

Ogistin knew better than to try to change his uncle's mind. Plaswa ordered Ogistin to set rabbit snares on the other side of the ridge that bordered their camp. Plaswa also gave John Stark several of the beaver traps that had been taken from him.

"You'll see a pond when you climb to the top of that hill," Plaswa told Ogistin. "There's a beaver dam there. Have John Stark set his traps at the pond." Ogistin picked up the traps and his gun while his uncle repeated the directions to the Pastoni. Plaswa handed John Stark a horn filled with beaver musk. Ogistin gestured to John Stark to lead the way up the hill.

They reached the pond quickly and found the beaver dam stretched across one end of it. Thin ice still covered its northern sections, but here on its southern banks, where the sun cut through the pine trees, there were open spots on the water.

Ogistin gave John Stark a trap and pointed to the pond. They walked along the bank while John Stark looked for an appropriate spot. He found what he was looking for: the prints of beaver paws and dragged tails in the soft mud, nibbled shoots, bits of fur caught in a branch. He sat down and took off his boots.

The Pastoni stepped into the pond and secured one end of the trap chain with a stick. He carefully pulled the trap apart, setting it under a few inches of water. He thrust a long twig into the mud so it would stick out of the water, just above the trap. John Stark then opened the horn and let a few sticky drops of musk fall on the end of the twig.

The strong musk odor would attract the beaver to the twig. When it paddled over to investigate, it would spring the trap. The beaver would dive and try to escape to deeper water, but it would be held fast by the chain. Eventually, it would tire of the struggle and drown.

John Stark set three traps around the southern half of the pond, then looked at Ogistin for further direction. The boy pointed the prisoner away from the hill, and after they'd walked a while, Ogistin stopped and gestured to a small opening beneath a log. He showed the Pastoni the rabbit droppings that marked the path the animal took.

Ogistin nudged John Stark away from the rabbit lair with his gun and motioned his prisoner to sit near a large tree about thirty paces away. Ogistin picked up two small logs and brought them over to a sapling near the rabbit den. He bent the young tree over so that the tops of its branches touched the ground on the other side of the den opening and placed the two logs on them to hold them down. Taking a cord made of deer sinew from his pouch, he tied one end to the center of the curved trunk of the sapling. He made a small noose at the other end of the cord. The noose barely touched the ground.

He carefully placed branches on either side of the noose. When the rabbit ran through the noose to go in or out of its den, it would spring the trap and the noose would tighten around the animal.

Ogistin half expected his prisoner to try to run off, but when he finished the snare, John Stark was just where he'd left him, looking intently at Ogistin's trap. Ogistin guessed he'd impressed the Pastoni with his abilities, and felt very clever.

He motioned to John Stark that they must move on. John Stark walked over to the trap and examined it carefully. Then the Pastoni picked up a stick, put it through the noose, and tugged.

11
Battle!

John was on the ground, scuffling with Ogistin, punching, kicking. John didn't care that ruining the snare was the act that finally made the boy snap. He hated the young hunter. He hated being a prisoner.

Ogistin fought with amazing power. Rocks, sticks, bits of ice scraped John's skin as they rolled over the wet ground. The two pushed each other into trees and shrubs.

John tripped Ogistin and jumped on his back.

Ogistin tried to get up. John held firm. Ogistin grabbed a stick and hit John on the side of the head. John weakened his hold. Ogistin jerked away, but John was on him again. He knocked the boy to the ground, pounced on him, grabbed his neck. He began to squeeze...

Suddenly John felt himself being lifted into the air. He turned and looked up into Lobal's huge face. John couldn't help being impressed. Lobal had easily lifted him up from the ground and held him back without effort. To his left, John saw Amos holding Ogistin. "Plaswa sent us to help you," Amos said, struggling to hold the boy. "I guess he figured he'd sent two fools out by themselves."

John's breath came in huge gulps, as he turned and glared at Ogistin. When John's arms were finally released, he rubbed his shoulders, his eyes never leaving Ogistin.

The boy jerked away from Amos. He picked up his musket, returning John's glare.

Lobal spoke to Ogistin and then motioned John and Amos back to camp.

"When's it going to stop, John?" Amos asked him. "You're a man, but you're acting no better'n the boy."

"He may be a boy, Amos, but he's still a savage, and he's not going to get me."

"And you're *not* a savage?"

"A man's got to stand up for himself."

"You weren't doing a very good job of it. We watched you for a while. You were reckless. Even I could see you weren't thinking straight."

"What're you saying? I *had* him, Amos."

"Sure you had him. For the moment. Ogistin had a rock the size of a small cannon ball in his hand when Lobal pulled you off. How much longer do you think you'd have lasted? He was about to crack your skull open."

John shook his head. "No. Didn't you see, Amos? He was weakening. If you'd helped me, we could've been free."

Amos raised both hands above his head. "Free to do what? Starve in the woods?"

"Better'n being prisoners." John growled. Amos stopped, his face inches away from John's. "We may be prisoners, Johnny, but this prisoner intends to get to St. Francis alive," he said and marched off ahead of John.

John fully expected some sort of punishment, but except for Lobal, who remained as guard, the camp was empty. Lobal left John to his own devices and began to work on a raccoon carcass.

Amos turned his back on John and went to help Lobal with the skinning.

Ogistin was nowhere around. John sat on the ground and picked up a small branch and began to peel the dry bark from it. He watched Amos use one of the Abenaki knives to skin a small raccoon. It was the first time either of them had been allowed to hold a weapon. John thought briefly of escape, but chuckled as he imagined he and Amos trying to hold off ten men with a skinning knife!

They weren't closely guarded, but both of them knew better than to try and run off. They wouldn't have been able to outrun the Abenaki. What Amos said was true: they could starve trying to get back to Derryfield.

Lobal put the raccoon meat on a drying rack over a low fire. The bones were put aside. The raccoon's brain went into a container and was covered with a bit of water. Lobal set the pot on the hot coals.

John could see a similar pot that held a kind of soup made from animal brains. Lobal made a paste of the brains and water. He and Amos smeared the paste over the raccoon hides with flat stones, rolled up the hides, and put them aside.

"That's about the way we do it too," John heard Amos tell Lobal. Amos was gesturing as he spoke, showing Lobal with actions as well as words that Lobal's method of preparing pelts was not much different from theirs. But, John thought, the Abenaki seemed better able to make tools from the simplest bits of wood and stone.

John had seen French and English traps and weapons in the camp. But the Abenaki didn't depend on these. During their long weeks of captivity, he and

Amos had often noticed how the Indians' ability to use things at hand allowed them to travel more lightly than any English trapper John could name.

These people might be resourceful, but still John concentrated on the fact that they were his enemies. Now, even Amos seemed to be turning against him. Did the fool think these Indians were going to let him go if he tried to act as if he were one of them?

Amos was letting himself forget that he was an Englishman. Not only were these men savages, they were allies of France! For as long as John could remember, the English had been fighting the French for control of the colonies. None of the peace treaties between the two countries seemed to last.

John vowed he wouldn't fall into the same trap Amos was getting into. It was up to him to keep the Abenaki guessing. As angry as he was at Amos and his sharp words, John determined he would watch out for his friend as well.

For two days after his fight with Ogistin, John did nothing. It would've made him feel better if his in-activity had been mentioned by someone. But the Abenaki paid no attention to him.

Once, John saw Ogistin come into camp with an armload of carcasses, but the boy went off again.

Maybe Plaswa was forcing him to stay away.

Amos continued to work with Lobal. Amos had even begun to pick up a few Abenaki words. How long had he been able to do this?

"Are you turning into one of them?" John asked his friend later.

Amos was still angry. "You can accuse me of turning Indian if you like. But I see it different. I see you doing nothing while I see me passing the time. We have no way to get out of this, so I'm going to make the best of it."

John didn't admit that he understood what Amos was saying. He had long thought of himself as an expert woodsman. Yet since being captured, he had learned a great deal more about surviving in the forest. Along with the traps and snares he had seen the Abenaki make, John had been amazed at some of the food he'd been given to eat since his capture. There were potatolike vegetables, dug up from the ground and boiled with whatever meat had been caught that day. There were early greens, sometimes poking out of the remaining snow patches. The greens were eaten raw or boiled to make a tea. The food might taste strange to John, but he was always hungry enough to eat anything.

Most of the time, the Abenaki contented themselves with the small portions that were usually available. But after a successful hunt, like when the group had brought back the deer, the men made huge stews and then ate until they could eat no more, many of them falling into deep sleep. They never seemed to worry about where the next meal might come from.

John shook his head. He didn't like the way his thoughts were heading. He was almost beginning to think like Amos. No matter what there was to admire in these people, he would not let himself forget one thing: they were his enemies.

Three days after the fight, Amos finally came to John: "Plaswa says we can check the trapline you set with Ogistin the other day. They want to move on. I'm willing—if you're done sulking."

John didn't reply. The truth was, he was bored. He was surprised to realize that he had become jealous of Amos's relationship with Lobal. But his pride wouldn't let him admit the truth.

"Well, we haven't got much choice, have we?" he said instead.

Lobal and the two Englishmen set out over the ridge and made their way to the pond. Each trap held a beaver.

"David couldn't have done better." Amos meant it as a compliment, but thinking of their friend saddened John.

They brought the carcasses back to camp and began to skin them.

"They are fine beaver, John Stark," Plaswa said as he came upon them. "They are yours to keep or trade."

John's head shot up. "What do you mean? Why are you letting me keep these pelts?"

"You set the traps," Plaswa said. "You caught the game, and now you are preparing the pelts. The beaver are yours."

John put down his skinning knife and stood up to face Plaswa. "But what about the pelts you took from us? My friends and I did all the work for those as well!"

"No, John Stark. You took the pelts that should have been ours."

"So *you* say. These beaver were caught on Abenaki land too."

"The difference is, I gave you permission. When you understand that difference, you will learn to respect the Abenaki."

12
Ogistin's Request

O gistin spent several days alone in the woods setting traps and skinning the animals he caught. He'd leave his catch in the camp and go off again. No one came looking for him. Plaswa would understand that he needed time to think.

The fight with John Stark had changed Ogistin. It hadn't lessened his hatred for the Pastoni prisoner. But it had shown him that he could lose. All this time, Ogistin had thought only about revenge. He hadn't thought about being beaten. What if Lobal and Amos Eastman hadn't arrived in time? Might John Stark have beaten him and run off? Or would he have killed John Stark with the rock, forgetting that Plaswa had made him responsible for the Pastoni life? Ogistin knew how close he'd come to that humiliation. He'd lost his head out of anger.

Plaswa had accused Ogistin of not doing his part on the hunt since the Pastoni had been taken prisoner. Even Kasko had reminded him of all the work they'd done last winter, trapping and hunting on their own, trying to earn the honor of being asked to join the Long Hunt. They collected pelts all winter, hoping to impress Plaswa and the other chiefs with their hard work. At the end of the summer, Plaswa had told them both to begin collecting extra ammunition and to make sure they each had a sharp skinning knife.

Plaswa had expected great things from Kasko and Ogistin. Ogistin now understood how right his uncle had been to accuse him of not doing his part since they'd captured the Pastoni.

Ogistin was determined to make up for his idleness. He ranged far from camp, setting snares and traps. He barely slept and ate little. By the time the moon was full, signaling the end of the hunting season, he'd contributed a good number of furs. Plaswa said nothing about the pelts. There was no need. Ogistin had simply done what was expected of him.

Ogistin met Kasko at the campfire, cleaning the last of the furs. He stopped his work to share some venison with Ogistin. "Plaswa says we're finished. We'll go home as soon as we're ready."

Ogistin nodded while he chewed. The pelts were ready to bring to the women. Toma had already finished making a sledge, which would be used to drag some of the bigger pelts until they reached Alsigôtêgok.

Ogistin stared at John Stark. The Pastoni was working on a beaver pelt. For a moment, Ogistin felt a vague sense of triumph. The Pastoni was finally behaving like a prisoner! He had won!

Kasko followed his gaze.

"The Pastoni caught several fat beaver in his traps. Plaswa is letting him keep the skins."

Ogistin stared at Kasko in disbelief.

"My uncle took the Pastoni prisoner. Now he lets him keep pelts as if he's one of the hunting party!"

Kasko shrugged. "It was a good catch. Plaswa honors John Stark's skill. It doesn't change anything. He's still a prisoner."

"So why do we honor a *prisoner?*"

Kasko didn't answer. Ogistin decided to find the one who had made the decision. It wasn't Ogistin's place to dispute any decision made by the Chief of the Hunt, but now the boy felt he could no longer be a part of those decisions.

"Nzasis." Ogistin addressed Plaswa as his uncle rather than as his leader.

Plaswa was busy melting lead for bullets. He didn't look up. "What is it, Ogistin?"

"Kasko says we'll be leaving soon."

"We've begun the preparations. The women will have started the planting by the time we return. Toma will go ahead and let them know we're coming."

"I'd like to go with Toma."

Plaswa's eyes narrowed a bit in surprise. "We need you here, Ogistin. There are many pelts."

"I'm strong, Nzasis. I can carry my load and keep up with Toma."

Plaswa studied Ogistin's face. If he understood that Ogistin needed to be away from John Stark, he didn't say it. His permission was given in the form of a warning:

"You must take your share of the pelts."

13
Hope

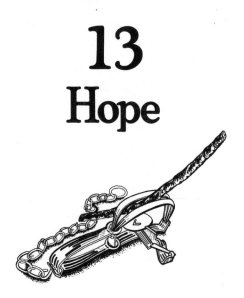

"Plaswa, where's Ogistin?" John asked.

"He has returned to St. Francis with Toma. When the rest of the pelts are ready, we'll follow."

So the young whelp was gone. John couldn't help feeling a bit smug. Plaswa must have tired of his nephew's antics and sent him off. That was great news. It could only mean they'd soon arrive in St. Francis.

The rhythm of camp work changed as everyone

made preparations to leave. Traps were brought in, pelts were tied in bundles, and food was prepared for the journey home.

"This is a good sign," John whispered to Amos as they sat, finishing their evening meal.

"What makes you say that? We're still heading *north,* Johnny." Amos kept his voice low.

"They'll let us go in St. Francis. You'll see."

Amos shook his head. "You're wrong. They've no reason to let us go. Why drag us all the way to St. Francis if they don't intend to sell us to the French?"

"I might have said the same a few days ago," John admitted, "but things have changed."

"What things?"

"Ogistin going off, for one. I think Plaswa sent him. And the beaver pelts he's let me keep. They're good skins. I think he's giving us something to have for trading. We could get at least one gun for them. That's all we need to get us back to Derryfield."

Amos shook his head. "I don't know. Something doesn't fit." He was quiet for a moment, then asked, "What day do you think this is?"

John shrugged. "I'm not sure. It's May or June, I think."

"Hard to tell this far north," said Amos. "The nights are cool."

"How long do you think we've been with them?" John asked. "Five weeks? Six?"

"More like six," Amos answered, licking the last bits of squirrel meat from his fingers. He sighed. "John, I miss cheese."

"And pie for breakfast, and my mother's bread and apple butter," John said. "Ma makes the best in Derryfield, I think."

Amos nodded. "And ale," he said. "A good tankard of ale." Amos let out a long sigh. "I hope your brother made it back there."

John stretched his arms and yawned. "Will's a good woodsman," he said. "He still had his knife."

"Nearly a hundred miles," Amos pointed out.

"Maybe he stopped in Stevenstown or Rumford. It'd be easy enough to canoe the Merrimack back to Derryfield after that." John refused to think Will might be dead.

Amos lay on his back and looked up into the sky. John poked at the fire. "Do you think we'll ever see it again, Johnny?"

"Derryfield? We'll be back there before the summer's over. We'll follow the rivers. That'll take us through the mountains fast enough. If we can't trade our pelts for a gun, maybe we can trade for a canoe. We ought to be able to scavenge enough food to get us back home."

"No," Amos said, "it'd be foolish to try the journey without a weapon. Better to trade for a gun. We could always build a raft for the rivers."

John and Amos kept their voices low. Planning their trip home gave them a bit of hope. Amos had one more question.

"Why do you think they'd bother with us this long just to let us go?"

John shrugged. "I figured *you'd* have an answer. You're the one that's become friendly with 'em."

Amos scowled. "I told you, I was just passing time. Anyway, that big one, Lobal, he didn't treat me too badly."

John turned his attention back to the fire. It was true, Lobal and Plaswa and the others had treated them pretty well during the journey. But Amos's question had brought doubts back into his mind. Something kept bothering him, kept sitting in the back of his thoughts like the memory of an old nightmare.

He remembered the night they had sat by the fire listening to Plaswa tell the story of the coming of the white people. "You say that this is not war," Plaswa had said, "but I tell you, it cannot be called peace. It has never been peace."

14
Homecoming

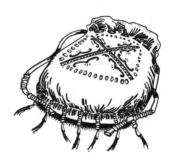

O gistin and Toma slept little, taking advantage of the lengthening spring days by traveling at an easy but steady pace.

"A few more days," Toma said, "and I'll see my new son."

Ogistin laughed. "What if your son is a daughter?"

Toma grinned. "I'll still be happy. But a few days from now Klalis and I will be together again and one way or another I *will* have a son!"

Ogistin understood how Toma felt. The closer they

were to St. Francis, the less Ogistin thought of John Stark and the more his thoughts turned to a certain young girl who had begun to smile at him last summer. O'zalik was the daughter of his mother's closest friend. Both families had been pleased when the young couple had begun to spend time together. The more O'gistin thought of O'zalik, the more anxious he became to learn if she had saved her smiles all winter.

Toma and Ogistin reached St. Francis within the week. They took turns dragging the sledge. When they reached Alsigôtêgok, they uncovered the dugout canoes they'd hidden so many weeks before. They transferred their load to the dugouts and traveled the water route to their village.

It didn't take long for the children of the village to spread word of their arrival. Soon several women were at the river's edge, taking the pelts from the hunters so the work of preparing them could go on.

Ogistin stood on the riverbank for a moment, taking in the familiar scenes. He could see a number of men fishing upriver. Some women tended the garden on the bluff. Ogistin searched the crowd for his family. O'zalik was nowhere to be seen.

Mali, though, had arrived to welcome her brother. She stood holding her young son's hand, laughing and greeting Ogistin.

"These are good pelts," Mali said, handing two

small ones to the boy. "Go, bring these to your grandmother," she urged her son. "Tell her Ogistin is home!"

"Nokemes, Nokemes!" the little one shouted as he struggled up the steep bank, "Ogistin is back!"

Ogistin and Mali smiled as they watched him run.

"When will the others arrive?" she asked.

"Two or three days, four at most. They brought down two bucks just before Plaswa decided to break camp. He let me come ahead with Toma."

His sister looked at him quizzically but did not press him for more information. "I'll take these to Mother," she said, following her son up the hill with an armful of pelts.

Toma handed up the last of their gear, and the two men dragged the canoes up onto the riverbank. They went to meet the village leaders to tell about the Pastoni prisoners who would soon arrive with Plaswa.

Ogistin couldn't stop looking all around the village. He'd forgotten, in these few months away, how wonderful St. Francis was. Cabin doors and shutters were open to let in the warm spring air. Welcoming voices and smiles followed the two hunters as they made their way across the village.

They greeted the Chief Speaker, Atecouando, where he sat outside his cabin.

"It was a good hunt, then?" Atecouando observed, nodding his head in the direction of some women who'd already begun to separate the pelts.

"A good hunt in many ways," Toma said. "Plaswa brings two Pastoni prisoners."

Toma told of capturing the two hunters, of the death of one and the other's escape. He spoke of Paslid's wound and described the furs the Abenaki had taken back from the Pastoni.

"And you, young Ogistin, how did you fare on your first Long Hunt?" Atecouando asked.

Ogistin answered quietly. "It was a good hunt. I hope my uncle will let me join him again." He also hoped his reply would satisfy Atecouando.

The Chief Speaker sent them off to join their families. Later the Council would discuss the issue of the Pastoni prisoners.

O'nis sat ouside her cabin waiting for her son. She hugged Ogistin and told Mali to get him something to eat. "Your father will return soon, I think," she said. "The fishing's still good. He's gone out with some of the others. I told him you'd come today."

Ogistin laughed. "How did you know? Did you get a sign? Are you becoming as wise as an old medawlinno?"

His mother went to one of the drying racks in front of the cabin. She forced a serious expression, but her eyes twinkled as she spoke. "I won't explain what you can't understand," she said as she turned the fish. "Even a sorcerer is allowed some secrets."

Mali laughed as she handed her brother a bowl. "You shouldn't tease him, Mother." She looked at Ogistin. "Mother's been telling Father for a week that each day was the day you'd come!"

Ogistin laughed and then took a sip of the fish stew. He told them about the trip and the capture of the Pastoni prisoners.

O'nis and Mali shared news of the village: this grandmother had died; that neighbor's young son was already learning to hunt with the men; some French had come to trade.

"And O'zalik asked about you." Mali glanced at her younger brother.

"She wasn't at the river when we arrived," Ogistin said crossly. He was annoyed that his sister was so aware of his feelings about O'zalik.

"She's gathering herbs with her father's sister," Mali answered.

"And now that you've returned from your great hunt, will you give O'zalik's mother the wampum string?" O'nis asked.

Ogistin scowled at his mother. "I will give the bride-gift at the proper time, Mother," he answered. "O'zalik is still a child."

"Not so much a child," Mali answered with a knowing smile.

Ogistin threw the empty bowl down in front of him and wiped his mouth impatiently with the back of his hand. "I've been gone for weeks and home for only a short while! Your home is already full, Mother!"

"There is always room for more grandchildren."

Ogistin threw up his arms. "I'm going to find my father! He won't bother me with such talk!" He pretended to storm off, glad to hear his mother and sister's laughter again.

Ogistin found Azô walking toward the village with a fine catch of fish.

Azô greeted his son warmly. "Your mother said you would come today."

"And every day for a week, I hear!"

"She missed her son," Azô said, handing Ogistin some of the gear. "It was a good hunt?"

"There'll be a lot to trade. Plaswa brings two Pastoni prisoners. They were trapping just below the White Hills. Plaswa wants to sell them to the French, I think."

"You've spoken to the Council?"

"Only to Atecouando. There were four, Father. One escaped."

"And the other?"

"Toma killed him." Ogistin opened his hunting pouch and handed his father the Pastoni scalp.

"Who took his scalp?"

"I did—for Simo."

Azô stopped walking and looked at Ogistin. "Your

brother has been dead many years, Ogistin. But I understand."

Ogistin clenched his fists. "If I'd been on that Long Hunt, he wouldn't have died. I could have helped him."

Azô looked up into the trees as if he were searching there for an answer to Ogistin's anger and pain. "For a long time, I felt that way too, Ogistin. When I'd hear your mother's soft crying, I'd think: I should have been there to protect our son and bring him safely home."

"Well, Father, now there is one less Pastoni to take from us. And one less Pastoni soul to haunt me."

15
Unsettled
Heart

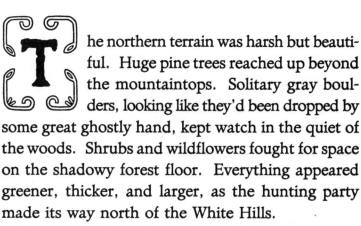

The northern terrain was harsh but beautiful. Huge pine trees reached up beyond the mountaintops. Solitary gray boulders, looking like they'd been dropped by some great ghostly hand, kept watch in the quiet of the woods. Shrubs and wildflowers fought for space on the shadowy forest floor. Everything appeared greener, thicker, and larger, as the hunting party made its way north of the White Hills.

John was restless. It wasn't only the concern over

what lay beyond this unfamiliar land. It was something more. Part of him wished that he were returning to Derryfield, yet part of him was drawn to St. Francis. He tried to explain his curious feelings to Amos.

"You miss the boy," Amos suggested.

"You're mad," John growled. He swatted a mosquito and rubbed his sleeve across his brow. When had it rained last? A week? Two weeks? He couldn't remember.

"I'm mad, am I?" Amos chuckled. "You've been sulking since he left. There's no one to challenge you now, and you need something to do."

"I've got something to do. I'm carrying this stinking pile of furs." John stopped suddenly, dropped the bundle, and removed his jacket. He tucked it into the pack and rehitched the bundle onto his back.

"Ah, maybe you're right, Amos." John shook his head. "In a way, it *was* easier when Ogistin was around."

"What do you mean?" Amos's voice was incredulous. "He never gave you a moment's peace."

John thought a moment before he answered. "But when he was here, I knew what I was fighting. Now a lot has changed. I've been thinking they could have treated us any way they wanted to. They could've beaten us or starved us or kept us tied up day and night. But they haven't done any of those things.

Would we have done the same?"

"I don't know."

"All the time you worked with Lobal preparing pelts, didn't you wonder why he let you do it? Didn't you wonder about that freedom?"

"What freedom?" Amos was waving his arms, barely controlling the level of his voice. "I told you, I was passing time. We couldn't escape. We'd have died in the woods one way or another with no food or weapons. What're you thinking, Johnny?"

"It's just this, Amos. When we were taken prisoner, I expected a great many things. But I can tell you what I didn't expect."

"And, what might that be?" Amos's voice betrayed his annoyance.

"I didn't expect to be treated so fairly."

They arrived in St. Francis in the early afternoon. Scouts had obviously announced their arrival, for a large group of people stood on the high bluffs, calling and waving to the hunters. There was ample help to unload the canoes and plenty of curiosity about the prisoners.

John and Amos followed their captors up the steep bank to an open area that seemed to serve as a sort of meeting place. One large building in the center was topped with a cross. Other, smaller cabins surrounded it in a sort of semicircle.

"This wasn't exactly the way I pictured it," John said to Amos under his breath.

Amos agreed. "These cabins look like the kind the French build."

John did some quick calculating. "More'n thirty cabins that I can see, and others beyond." He looked at the large gardens that had been planted farther upriver.

"I didn't expect it to be this crowded," said Amos.

John nodded. Women and children greeted the men and took the rest of their bundles to various homes. The fresher meat was hung on long drying racks built over smoky fires. Many of the racks were already filled with fish and other meat.

Little children ran about, laughing, playing, chasing dogs and each other. Neighbors waved to the returning men and then continued their work in the village or gardens. Older men and women sat smoking and talking outside some of the homes.

John saw Lobal and Kasko greet an elderly woman. Plaswa scooped up a tiny girl, put a finger on her cheek, and whispered in her ear.

"This one belongs to my eldest daughter," Plaswa explained proudly. "She was my shadow before we left on the hunt. Now she is not sure she remembers me. Weeks are a lifetime to babies."

John had never thought of his enemies as being capable of such tenderness. Until his capture, he had only met Indians in a fight or when he was trading. For the first time in his life, John looked at the Abenaki as men like himself: men with homes and families.

Some young children came and stood close by John and Amos, staring at the strangers. Amos chuckled and crouched down to their level.

"Ow!" Amos suddenly bellowed. The children scattered.

"What're you doing, frightening the little ones, Amos?" John teased.

Amos stood up and rubbed his jaw. "Me scare them? One of 'em just yanked my beard!"

John laughed out loud. "Didn't think you'd have to defend yourself against babies, did you?"

John and Amos were led to an area just on the edge of the half-moon of cabins. The children followed. Two young men were put in charge of guarding John and Amos. They looked to be a bit younger than Ogistin or Kasko.

"I don't see the boy," John said.

"Ogistin? Don't start that again, Johnny! Look, you were right, Plaswa *has* treated us well these last weeks. Don't go after more trouble with that whelp."

"I just want to know where he is. I don't want any surprises."

A bearded old man in a dusty black robe walked purposefully toward them.

"Oh no," Amos moaned, "the first white man we see in weeks, and he's a priest. I forgot the Indians were Papists. Looks like we'll be fighting for our souls as well, Johnny."

The old man spoke to their guards and then turned to John and Amos. "I am Joseph Aubery," he said in a heavy French accent. "You are called...?"

John and Amos introduced themselves.

"Do you live here, Aubery?" Amos asked.

"I came to St. Francis over thirty years ago."

"Then," John ventured, "maybe you know what they plan to do with us."

"I expect you will be sold."

"I don't suppose you'd be willing to speak for us?" Amos asked. "You know, one white man for another?"

Aubery nodded thoughtfully. "That would depend." He stretched out his hands, palms up. "I'm always willing to speak for one who is a member of my flock."

"You mean if we converted, don't you? If we renounced the Church of England?" Amos's voice was getting louder.

The old man smiled. "I am simply saying, Monsieur Eest-mohn, that I always defend those who follow the true faith."

"We won't do that, Aubery, and you know it,"

John said. "We're not about to renounce the King."

"Ah, but English kings were once the servants of the Pope as well. Until Henry VIII turned from the Church, we were all of one faith. Would you be renouncing your English king or simply returning to the faith of your ancestors?"

"None of your tricks, Papist!" Amos said. "The Church of England is just fine with me."

"I did not come here to, as you say, trick," the priest said calmly. "I came only to see if I could be of any help to you. I care for all the people of St. Francis—in any way I can." He bowed to them and walked away.

They watched him in silence. Finally, Amos said, "So, Johnny. How much hope do you have now?"

16
Atecouando Speaks

T he villagers gathered outside in the early evening to celebrate the hunters and their successes, and decide what should be done with the Pastoni.

The fresh fish and early vegetables would provide enough for a feast. Every family brought a share. Père Aubery blessed the food and said a prayer of thanksgiving for the hunters' safe return, while asking for the swift healing of Paslid's leg. The younger children ran about, playing games and eating when they wished. The adults, and the young people who considered themselves adults, sat together talking, joking, and eating.

Ogistin and Kasko sat with Plaswa and Toma. Kasko ate almost greedily, wiping the bottom of his bowl with a piece of bread.

"You're not eating, Ogistin. Here, have some bread. My mother made it with the last of the corn. I forgot how good it was." He broke off a piece, and Ogistin took it without looking at it.

Ogistin's mind wasn't on the food, but on the two men who sat outside the gathering. Kasko nudged him. Ogistin smiled distractedly and bit into the bread.

"You're right. It is delicious."

Kasko looked at him quizzically. "What are you thinking about? The Pastoni? They'll be gone soon. Put them out of your mind."

As if he'd heard Kasko's words, Atecouando stood up and announced, "It's time to discuss the winter hunt. Those who wish to speak may do so."

"Plaswa should speak first," said Toma.

"Yes, tell about the hunt," someone else called out.

"Nearly everyone has already heard about it," Plaswa said.

"It's a good tale, worth retelling," Azô insisted. Others echoed Azô's sentiments.

Plaswa stood up. He looked around at his friends

and family members, and took a moment to collect his thoughts. When he spoke, he began quietly: "The snow remained thick throughout most of the hunt. Grandmother Earth made it simple for us to track the animals. We took many furs, even in the early part of the hunt."

"They're fine furs, too!" Pidianske, Plaswa's wife, cut in. "They'll be worth a great deal when they're traded." Everyone laughed. No one took offense at her directness. She was proud of her husband. Even Plaswa smiled at her before continuing: "The weather held until we were just south of the White Hills. There we could feel the change in the season. We planned to begin the trip home and finish the hunt on the way when we saw signs that Pastoni hunters were nearby. They had been taking meat and furs from the Abenaki."

Atecouando puffed on his pipe and nodded. "Tell about the signs, Plaswa."

"We found Pastoni traps and the remains of the animals. The meat and bones were left to rot in the sun."

Ogistin looked at the other adults in the gathering. Some sat patiently listening to Plaswa's tale, but others, those who had lost members of their families in the wars, nodded when Plaswa spoke.

His uncle went on: "We decided to take the men prisoner. The first, John Stark, was taken easily.

He was unarmed and had been checking his traps. We knew there were others, but when we questioned him, he tried to lead us away from his friends. His tricks didn't work. His friends signaled for him, and we found three others.

"We were able to take one other prisoner. One man escaped, and another was shot by Toma when he tried to run. We were able to take all of the pelts they collected—furs that are rightfully ours. In our party, only Paslid was injured. He has borne his leg wound bravely, and it is healing well."

The hunters were warmly praised—especially Paslid and Toma. Ogistin sat, listening to the compliments, feeling ashamed that Plaswa had had to speak to him on the hunt about his behavior.

Azô spoke: "My son, Ogistin, has more to tell."

All eyes faced Ogistin. Kasko smiled at him. Although he hadn't expected his father's comment, Ogistin understood that this was the time to display the scalp. He quietly opened Simo's hunting pouch and removed the scalp.

There were murmured comments, but Azô went on: "The Pastoni thief was dead when my son took the scalp. Ogistin avenged his brother Simo in his own way, and I'm proud of him."

"The boy did well!" someone shouted.

An old woman hissed in Ogistin's ear: "You captured the Pastoni's spirit!"

Toma took the scalp from Ogistin and said, "As a boy, I listened to the stories the old ones told of the good life they led at the foot of the White Hills. The Pastoni need to know what we've lost and what we protect." Toma shook the scalp as he spoke, gesturing toward the prisoners.

"Do you propose another war, Toma?" Père Aubery asked.

"No, Patlihôz. I don't wish to fight another war because of two men. But these two must pay for their thievery with more than the loss of their pelts." He held the scalp up in the air. Some of the younger men shouted agreement with Toma's words. Older people commented more quietly. Ogistin stood up.

"I'd like to speak, Atecouando."

The Chief Speaker signaled the Council's permission. The young man looked into the faces of the people of his village—friends and family and others who had been forced to seek shelter in St. Francis after the Pastoni destroyed their villages.

"I don't have the wisdom of the old," he began. "But I've listened to many stories of how strong the People once were.

"When our hunting party found the Pastoni hunters, I knew I was feeling all of the things Simo felt before he was murdered. The Pastoni who killed my brother didn't say, 'This one's a young hunter. We'll let him live.' They saw Simo's weapon and the color of his skin, and for these he was killed."

Ogistin paused and looked directly at Plaswa.

"I ask my uncle's forgiveness. Once we took the two prisoners, I wasn't a good hunter. I was a child seeking revenge. But I didn't see two men. I saw two *Pastoni* men. I heard their speech and knew it was the kind of talk my brother heard before he died. I saw their clothing and knew it was the kind of clothing my brother saw before the Pastoni killed him. We should never have taken these prisoners. We should've cut out their hearts and left them for the wolves to finish off."

The gathering was silent. Ogistin sat down and looked to Atecouando for a reply. Instead, Plaswa spoke. "My nephew's anger shouldn't be ignored. He said what was in his heart."

Atecouando nodded. The other council members murmured comments to him. Finally, a decision was made. Atecouando stood to address the crowd. "These men are certainly worth most to us alive. This is what the Council says: The Pastoni will be sold to the French. But first, let's see what kind of men these Pastoni are. Are they cowards, or is there some courage in their hearts? Tonight, let them run the course."

The villagers cheered. If the Pastoni ran the course bravely, then their capture would be an honor to the members of the hunt.

"Come, Azô! Play for us!" one villager urged. Ogistin's father unhitched a large rattle from his waist. A few other men joined him. They sang a song of celebration, a song to honor the ten men who had returned safely. The crowd quickly formed a circle, and the dancing began.

17
The Gauntlet

"It is decided. You will be sold." Plaswa stood above John and Amos, holding long poles decorated with feathers and small pelts.

Amos let out a sigh. "My father's tale doesn't seem so foolish now, does it, Johnny? Those few beaver pelts won't buy both of us our freedom. Who knows how long it'll take us to get back after all!"

"But we're alive, Amos. Remember, you said as much before. We're still better off than David."

"What's this?" Amos asked as Plaswa held out the poles. They were cut from young trees, nearly six feet long.

"Hold it in front of you," Plaswa answered, "when you run the course."

"What do we have to do?" Amos's voice sounded high-pitched and frightened. John looked steadily at Plaswa. "It's the gauntlet, isn't it, Plaswa?"

"I have heard some Pastoni call it by that name."

Amos's head snapped around, and he looked at John. His eyes were wide and tight. They both knew running the gauntlet was an old practice used among many tribes to test a captive's courage.

"You will be first, Amos Eastman," Plaswa said. Amos stared at the pole but didn't reach for it. Plaswa held it out until Amos took it, hesitantly. John took his as well. There was nothing more to do but wait. He looked at the crowd and saw Ogistin talking to Toma. It seemed the boy had won after all.

Plaswa turned to leave. "I will return for you."

The villagers continued their celebration. The sound of rattles made pleasant rhythms to accompany the singers. People of all ages danced around the musicians. Some dances looked like simple two-steps. Others were more complicated and beautiful. John watched, fascinated. He felt he could understand some of the stories the songs and movements represented.

When the music and dancing finally stopped, people milled around chatting and resting. The sky, a deep rose color, predicted its own future. Tomorrow would be another beautiful day. John wondered if he even cared what the future would bring.

Plaswa returned, and the young guards poked their muskets at John and Amos, forcing them toward the crowd. They were brought before a smaller group of important-looking men and women. These people were the Village Council, Plaswa explained, the decision makers. He introduced John and Amos to Atecouando, the Chief Speaker.

Atecouando looked to John to be about his pa's age. Two large, brown feathers were knotted to the side of his long, graying hair. Atecouando wore leggings, a breechcloth, and a vest. A necklace of braided strips of leather was ornamented by a cockade, which John suspected might have once decorated the uniform of an English officer.

Atecouando was brief. Plaswa translated his short statement. "You are to be punished for your theft, Pastoni."

"That's all of it?" Amos cried. "We get no chance to speak?"

"This isn't an English trial, Amos," John said. "It seems our crime and punishment have already been decided."

"What have you to say, Pastoni?" Plaswa asked.

"We have told our Council everything. What does it matter if you tell the tale? Is it not one story?"

"Your chief needs to hear our side of it."

"Let them speak."

John and Amos whirled around, surprised to hear their own language from Atecouando.

"Why keep us here, Atecouando?" John asked. "We did nothing to the people of St. Francis."

"Then tell me, Pastoni, where were you when our men took you prisoner?"

"You know the answer to that, Atecouando," Amos cut in, "below the White Hills." He shook the pole he held in awkward, angry movements. For a second, John thought Amos was going to throw it. He could see that his friend was becoming more frightened and angry.

"English surveyors told us that the land was the property of the Crown," John said quietly. He gripped his stick with one hand and left the other free, ready to grab at Amos if he made a move.

"And who has given these men permission to measure our lands?" Atecouando asked. "It is not by agreement with the Abenaki."

Atecouando looked around at the people who sat on either side of him before he went on. "When the last peace came, we hoped to enjoy it with our French brothers," he said. "We had lost many, including four of our young hunters who were killed just before the peace was signed. Since then, another of our men has been killed in the winter. And now a Pastoni woman who married a man from our village has told us she witnessed the murder of an Abenaki man and woman by the Pastoni. How can this be when we are at peace and are honoring our agreements with your Governor?"

"We had nothing to do with those murders, Atecouando!" Amos yelled. John put a hand on his friend's shoulder and squeezed it gently.

"The chief doesn't hold us here because of the murders, Amos," John said. "You've got your revenge for that, haven't you, Atecouando?"

"Your friend is dead because he tried to run, John Stark," Plaswa answered instead. "He could have been here with you."

The priest, who had been sitting quietly behind Atecouando, spoke up. "The Abenaki do not need a life for a life, Monsieur Stark. That is *English* justice."

"And how do the English punish theft?" Atecouando asked.

"You must pay for what you stole. If you can't, there's debtors' prison," John answered.

"Then you have said it for yourself," Atecouando said. "You must pay for your theft. You will be sold to the French."

"But what of this?" Amos asked, shaking the pole

in front of him. "This has nothing to do with our so-called theft. Why don't you just sell us, Atecouando, and be done with it?"

"No, you do not run the course to pay for your theft," Atecouando agreed. "You do it to prove your courage. Tomorrow, our friend Gamelin will be here. He always needs workers for his mill and will be happy to buy you. But tonight, you will honor our hunters by proving yourselves."

The crowd began to organize itself. The women formed two lines. The men and the children stood off to the right. Atecouando and the rest of the elders stayed to the left. Voices were low. The sound of a baby crying nearby seemed unusually loud in the hushed gathering.

Plaswa took Amos first and led him to the front of the lines of women. He showed Amos how to hold the pole before him as he walked.

Plaswa nudged Amos forward, and Amos walked between the lines, the pole jerking in front of him as he made his way. Each woman touched Amos on the shoulder, back, or head as he walked between them. When he reached the end, he was led back to stand near John.

No one spoke as Plaswa signaled that it was John's turn. John walked stiffly between the women's rows, keeping his eyes straight ahead. How could this simple ceremony prove his courage to the Abenaki?

John's question was answered when the men then formed their lines. John looked at their faces. Toma was there, and even the large, gentle Lobal. Kasko, nearly as tall as his father, stood near Lobal. Kôgôwes and Paslid from the hunting party were there too.

There were many faces he didn't recognize. But when he saw the first one in line, John gripped the pole so tightly his fingernails dug into the wood.

Ogistin.

The youth held a small, thick stick in his right hand. Sweat shone on his face and arms.

Plaswa led Amos to the front of these new lines. Another Abenaki stood on Amos's left. The two men placed their hands on Amos's shoulders.

Amos gripped the pole. His eyes seemed to bulge, and his breaths were long and loud. Plaswa and the other man pushed Amos forward.

Amos ran as fast as he could, trying to shield his face, but the long pole made it difficult to do either. John watched the fists and clubs land on his friend's head and back, and he relived all the pain he'd felt on the day they'd been captured. He heard Amos grunt once or twice. The sound of Amos's boots thudding across the ground mixed with the sounds of the blows.

The run seemed to last forever, though John knew it had only been a matter of seconds.

Amos lay on the ground, moaning, the pole still

clutched in one hand. His face was already beginning to swell from his beating, and blood was seeping
from a gash over one eye. Two of the men dragged
Amos away to a small cabin behind the church.

Now it was John's turn.

Plaswa and the other man brought him to the front
of the lines. Ogistin looked at John and raised his
wooden club above his head in readiness. John didn't
flinch from the boy's stare but picked up his pole and
held it in front of him.

He made his decision. He would fight Ogistin in
any way he could.

18
A Captive's Revenge

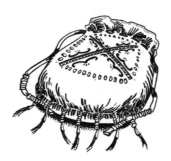

ohn Stark represented everything Ogistin found in the Pastoni to hate. From the first, he'd fought John Stark to make up for the loss of his brother. But since coming home, Ogistin had thought a lot about the things his father had said. He wasn't fighting John Stark only to avenge Simo. He fought to prove to himself that he was strong and that neither he nor any more of his family would die at the hands of a Pastoni.

Ogistin raised his club. Plaswa placed his hands on John Stark's shoulders. Just as Plaswa began to push John Stark forward, the Pastoni bolted *toward* the double line with full force, yelling a charge: "Aaaaaaaaahhh!"

Before Ogistin could react, he saw the long pole swing toward him and felt it bash the side of his head. He brought down his arms to protect himself, dropping his club. He bent to pick it up, but it was too late to fight back.

John Stark ran through the line striking at everyone he could. The pole cracked, but the prisoner kept swinging it while running, screaming and attacking like an angry bear.

Ogistin could see the other men in the lines reacting as he had. Some tried to fight back. Others attempted to block the Pastoni's blows, but it all happened too quickly. No one stopped John Stark. They hadn't been ready. They had expected this prisoner to be as docile as the first one.

Ogistin saw his enemy at the far end of the line turn and face the crowd. He was breathing heavily, holding the broken pole above his head, and staring down the lines of men. No one moved.

They all stared at him. For a few moments, it was nearly silent. The quiet was broken by John Stark's raspy breathing, someone's cough.

Then Atecouando began to laugh. The Chief

Speaker was nodding his head and pointing to the prisoner saying, "Well done! Well done! That one's very brave. He's cunning and gives a good fight!" Soon others joined in: "Yes! A brave man! An honor to the hunters!"

Plaswa grinned. Lobal rubbed his head and smiled. Even Kasko sat on the ground and joined in with his own chuckles.

But to Ogistin, the laughter sounded like taunting. The Pastoni had bested him. And instead of being angry, the villagers were laughing and complimenting the man who had stolen from them!

Ogistin was furious. He threw down his club and stormed away from the village. He stopped only long enough to take his gun from his father's cabin.

19
The Council's Decision

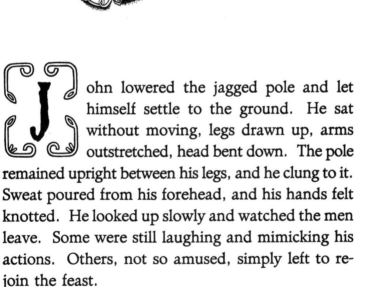

John lowered the jagged pole and let himself settle to the ground. He sat without moving, legs drawn up, arms outstretched, head bent down. The pole remained upright between his legs, and he clung to it. Sweat poured from his forehead, and his hands felt knotted. He looked up slowly and watched the men leave. Some were still laughing and mimicking his actions. Others, not so amused, simply left to rejoin the feast.

John looked for Ogistin but couldn't see him.

The musicians took out their rattles, and the rhythms called everyone to sing and dance once again. John's breathing slowed, and he felt very tired. He let the pole drop and stretched his fingers to get the feeling back in his hands. He rested his head on his knees, wondering what to do next.

When he lifted it, a young girl was standing in front of him, shyly holding out a bowl of food. As soon as he took the bowl, she ran back to the crowd. John sipped the fish stew slowly, allowing himself time to think.

He decided he was only slightly worse off than he'd been earlier in the day. Though he could still try to run off, he couldn't leave Amos. His friend was in no condition to travel.

Plaswa walked up to John. "Atecouando wishes to speak with you." He waited while John slowly got to his feet. They made their way back to the council members. The Chief Speaker sat with other older men and women and the priest. John was told to sit by their small fire.

"You fought well, Pastoni," Atecouando said. "Courage is a good thing, is it not?"

"Yes." John didn't know what else to say.

"Where is your home?"

"I come from Derryfield, in the New Hampshire colony."

"That village is near a great river."

"We call it the Merrimack," John said.

"My father was a Pennacook. His people lived along that river before they came here. This was many years ago."

When John didn't answer, Atecouando went on. "Tell me, John Stark, do the fish still come in great numbers to that river each spring?"

John nodded. "The men in my town sometimes fight each other for the best fishing spots."

The old man laughed, and John chuckled a bit nervously. "Yes, it must be so," Atecouando said. "My father told tales of the great number of fish that came to the river in the spring. When he was a boy, people would come from many villages to fish and feast. Even the villages that were enemies would make peace during this time. There was plenty for all."

"The old men in Derryfield say the river was once black with fish," John said. "Some say, in the spring, you couldn't dip your hand in the water without bringing up a fish." It seemed odd, swapping tales with this man.

Atecouando spoke to the others in the group. John waited impatiently to learn what was being discussed. He heard his name and saw the others nodding in agreement.

"You will stay with us, John Stark. We will speak again," Atecoundo said finally.

Plaswa took John's arm. "Come," he said.

John was confused. "The chief has told me to stay."

Atecouando nodded. "Yes. You will stay in the village."

"Do you mean we won't be sold, Atecouando?"

"You amuse us, Pastoni," Atecouando said, "but we have no use for your friend. The Council has decided."

John was led away before he could say more. He begged to see Amos, but Plaswa refused. Instead he took John through the crowd of dancers, then between a tiny cabin and the church.

"Is Amos all right, then?" John asked.

"Amos Eastman will survive, John Stark," Plaswa said. He pointed to the little cabin they'd just passed. "He is there, in the priest's house. Père Aubery will tend his wounds. And the mill owner, Gamelin, is not as bad as some of the men that come to us for slaves. He allows them to buy back their freedom after a time."

"Won't you speak for Amos, Plaswa? Ask your chief to keep him too."

"Why, John Stark? Do you think you will be better off than your friend? Amos Eastman will be among his own kind at least. But you must always remember that you are here at the whim of the Council." Plaswa walked up to one of the larger cabins.

"This is my home. You will stay with us." Plaswa entered the cabin ahead of John.

John stopped and looked back towards the priest's house. He wondered when he would see his friend again.

20
Full Circle

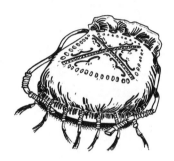

Dusk turned to dark, but Ogistin kept walking, guided by the light of the waning moon. When he finally stopped, it was only to sip a drink from a small stream. He sat on his knees, wiped his mouth with the back of his hand, and looked around. There were some changes to the place, but Ogistin knew where he was. He hadn't been back since the winter when he'd waited for his guardian spirit. He remembered the shelter he'd made, the cold and hunger he'd felt, and finally, the appearance of Bezo.

He walked a few yards away from the stream and saw a familiar gray boulder. A little more to the west would have been, yes, there it was: the tree on which he'd leaned the cedar boughs to make his shelter. The tree was rotting and cracked, but one end was still caught between the two smaller trees—grown wider and taller than he remembered.

He sat and looked at the scene. He lay his gun over his lap, leaned his head back, and closed his eyes. At this moment, he felt more at home here than in his own village. The others should have stood up to the Pastoni instead of laughing at John Stark's antics.

But I won't have to deal with the Pastoni again, Ogistin decided. Gamelin will buy the two prisoners and take them away to his mill.

He stretched his legs and crossed his arms. He was finished with John Stark.

The next morning, Ogistin followed the stream north to a deep spot where he knew he'd find fish. Using his knife, he fashioned a spear from a tree branch and leaned over the bank, searching the dark spots for movement. He managed to spear a medium-sized trout.

It didn't take him long to set up a fire and cook

his catch. For the first time in weeks, Ogistin relaxed.

He returned the fish bones to the brook and thanked the fish for giving its life for him. He doused his fire, picked up his gun, and began to explore the area farther north of his old camp.

The ground rose up into a small, rocky hill. He recalled that after Bezo had come into his shelter, he'd followed the lynx's tracks to this spot. But he hadn't wanted to hunt Bezo. He'd tracked the cat out of curiosity and then left it alone, anxious to return home. But now he was drawn to this place. He thought he knew where the cat might have a den—if no French trappers had found the spot.

The front of the hill was gray, nearly straight rock. Ogistin walked around behind it. The back sloped gently and was wooded. He climbed to the top, looked out, and saw smoke from the fires in St. Francis.

Then Ogistin went around to the west side of the hill. He climbed midway down the rock face, but couldn't go any farther. He scanned chiseled places in the rock, but could see no hole or outcrop big enough to be Bezo's den. He turned, disappointed. Perhaps he didn't understand his guardian spirit as well as he thought.

As he made his way back up the slope, he brushed against a small white spruce that had managed to grow in a crevice. Its needles scraped his arm, and as he pushed the branch out of the way, something caught his eye. A hole, hardly wider than the butt of Ogistin's musket, had been hidden by the scraggly spruce.

Ogistin carefully pulled the small tree aside and peered into the hole. At first he saw nothing, but he let his eyes adjust. Two pairs of tiny yellow eyes were staring back at him. Quietly, Ogistin let the tree fall back in place. He scrambled up the hill and looked around quickly. Cubs meant that the mother would be nearby.

He went around the back of the hill and worked his way down through the woods until he was facing the front of the outcrop again. He climbed atop a boulder at the foot of the hill and lay on his stomach, facing the cliff. Ogistin shielded his eyes and tried to locate the little spruce tree that marked the opening to the den.

He didn't know how long he lay, waiting for Bezo. He might have dozed; he wasn't sure. But he was suddenly aware that he'd been staring for some time at a part of the rock that seemed to move. The lynx came into focus as she dragged a large hare toward the spruce tree. It was all Bezo could do to hang on to it and cling to the rock face.

Just as the lynx was about to enter her den, Ogistin

saw a flash of red-orange above her, on the top of the hill. A fox held its nose to the air. One little kit danced awkwardly at its mother's feet.

Wôkwses could smell Bezo but couldn't see her yet.

Ogistin watched, fascinated. Bezo and Wôkwses were mortal enemies. What would Bezo do to this threat so close to her young?

Bezo dragged the rabbit into her den but returned immediately. The cat stood poised to chase the fox. Wôkwses stared back, then picked up her pup by its scruff and disappeared over the top of the hill. Bezo returned to her den.

"The fox is your enemy, Bezo, yet you let her go! I don't understand," Ogistin whispered.

He stared for a while longer at the scraggly spruce in the rock face, before he turned to go back to his old camp. It was just one more thing, he decided, that didn't make any sense.

Ogistin roamed the woods for two days, hunting small game for his meals and waiting for his anger to pass. It rained on the second day, the only rain he remembered in weeks. The rain seemed to make the withered plants turn greener almost as Ogistin watched. He turned toward home, enjoying the warm, gentle water on his head, face, and back.

He arrived in the early morning and found his mother sitting in the doorway, crushing dried herbs. Ogistin handed her some squirrel pelts. "These will make fine boots for your sister's youngest one."

O'nis looked at his face. "Your wound is nearly healed."

He scowled at her. "I'm not a child, Mother. I don't need your concern."

"Yes, I know. My son is a man now. But I didn't stop being a mother when you reached adulthood. My concern for you is my right, Ogistin." She frowned.

He sat across from his mother and let out a breath. Ogistin watched her long, smooth hair wave back and forth with the action of her arms.

"I'm sorry, Mother. I thought I'd left my anger behind."

"You felt the Pastoni humiliated you."

"But he did!"

"Was your injury greater than anyone else's or more important? Why should you feel shame because the Pastoni didn't let you beat him? Would you have let others hurt you without a fight? It's just as well that he did fight. What kind of honor was it for you or my brother to have captured an unarmed man? At least now you know the Pastoni's worth."

"I've thought of all those things, Mother. But I've never hated another man as much as John

Stark." He hesitated. "I can't explain."

"Because it's not only hate you feel. It's anger and fear and many other things."

Ogistin looked up sharply. "I'm not afraid of the Pastoni."

"My son is brave," his mother agreed. "You don't fear battle, Ogistin, because you can see what you're fighting. But the Pastoni are clever. They take from the Abenaki even when they claim to be giving."

"They took your son, Mother."

"Yes, and I could waste my time, Ogistin, thinking of what my life might have been like. My great-grandfather was an elder of the Pigwacket people, and my grandfather was honored as a skillful hunter. My mother was just learning our stories when the Pastoni came and destroyed our village, and the elders were killed. So much of what my mother could have learned was lost."

O'nis paused and stared upward, gathering her thoughts. "And I can still remember, even though I was just a child myself, seeing your father and his family arriving in our village. Your father had seen only nine summers. His father had been killed with the Penobscot chief, Paugus, as they fought to defend their village.

"If I dwell on all these things," O'nis said sadly, "and tally the wrongs the whites have done to our family alone, I'd have enough fuel to feed my anger forever. But I can't live my life in anger, Ogistin."

"I can," Ogistin shot back. "My anger will help me keep the Pastoni from doing more harm to our people."

O'nis looked down and continued to grind the herbs. "Then make your anger useful, Ogistin. Use everything you have to learn about the Pastoni. What has my brother taught you all these years?"

Ogistin looked up to the sky, impatient with this ridiculous question. "He's taught me to hunt."

O'nis stopped her work and shook her head. "No. Plaswa taught you to use your eyes and ears and nose. He taught you to learn each animal's habits. You became a successful hunter once you knew those things."

Ogistin nodded and took his mother's hand, remembering when it was his hand that had fit into hers. O'nis looked into his eyes. "Learn the Pastoni ways to use *for* us—and *against* them when there's danger. Use all your senses. Simo didn't have that opportunity. You do."

"Maybe I'll have that chance someday." Ogistin released his mother's hand and stood up to put his musket in the cabin. "The Pastoni are gone now."

Ogistin's mother reached out to stop him, "Ogistin," she said, "you left before the Council's decision. Atecouando sold only one Pastoni. The Council decided to keep the one called John Stark."

21
Left among the Enemy

ohn never saw Amos leave the village. He heard that his friend had been sold but was told little else. He wished, now, that he'd tried harder to convince Amos to try and escape.

Maybe not, he thought as he sat on the ground just outside Plaswa's cabin eating a simple breakfast of tea and fried johnnycake. He had to be honest. He and Amos would have had to go through too much unfamiliar territory. It had taken about six weeks to reach St. Francis from the Pemi River, with all the stops the hunting party had made. Even if he and Amos had traveled day and night, it would have taken at least half that long to get home.

"Amos was right, we'd have starved to death," he said to himself. But what Plaswa had said was true. He wasn't necessarily better off. He still had to deal with Ogistin.

John hadn't seen the boy during the two days since the feast. He'd been with Ogistin long enough to expect that there'd be a price to pay when he returned.

Officially, John was under the Council's protection, but Ogistin could get to him if he chose to. John never allowed himself to relax. He didn't want Ogistin to catch him off guard. For two days, he'd barely slept, waking at the tiniest sound. He spent hours in Plaswa's dark, cramped house. John had been given a makeshift pallet of blankets in one corner of the hot, dim room.

On the second day, rain had forced the family indoors. The shutters had been drawn to keep the rain out. The only light came from the fire. He sat, watching Plaswa's family, feeling as much like a prisoner as if he'd been thrown in a dungeon.

Pidianske and her daughters prepared food and clothing. Plaswa and his son went out to fish. In the afternoon, Plaswa cleaned or repaired his weapons. In the evening, the family talked while they did handiwork or played games of chance with painted stones.

But here, at least, John felt safe. Ogistin couldn't get him in Plaswa's house. There was only one door to watch.

On the third day, when the sun returned, John took his breakfast outdoors. He watched all sides as he left the cabin. He found a dry spot near the front door and sat with his food set on his lap. When he finally did see Ogistin, the boy didn't notice him. Ogistin and Kasko, spears in their hands, walked toward the river and disappeared over the steep bank.

Plaswa came to sit by John.

"Plaswa, what does Atecouando plan to do with me?" John asked him.

"Atecouando does not make any plans," Plaswa explained. "He only speaks for the Council. When the Council decides, they'll tell us." Pidianske brought Plaswa fried bread and a bowl of tea. A little girl scrambled up on Plaswa's lap. John recognized her as the one Plaswa had called his shadow. Plaswa dipped the edge of the bread in the tea and offered it to the child. She took a bite and smiled up at him, crumbs and drops of tea clinging to her chin.

"I need to do something, Plaswa. I can't sit here watching babies run around for another day. Will the Council at least let me work?"

"I will ask."

"Work would help pass the time."

Plaswa finished his meal and left. As John waited for Plaswa's return, he looked at his surroundings, remembering how the sight of the cabins had surprised him just days before. He didn't know what he'd expected exactly. Ragged, bowl-shaped wigwams? A small, half-starved band of Indians? St. Francis was nothing like that.

Only one thing in the village caused John to shudder: tall poles stood in front of some of the homes. Like the poles from the gauntlet ceremony, they were decorated with colorful feathers and animal furs, but several held something else—scalps.

He scowled, thinking of David, wondering if his family knew and if Will had made it back home.

John forced his thoughts elsewhere. He stretched, glad to be outdoors once again. At night, sleep pallets covered nearly every inch of floor space in Plaswa's crowded home. Plaswa had several young children, and two of Plaswa's older daughters had brought their young men to live with the family. John had learned that it was the custom for the engaged couple to live one year with the girl's family. At the end of the year, a formal marriage ceremony would take place, and the couple would move to their own home.

"Père Aubery does not approve," Plaswa had said after he'd introduced his family. "But the man has no wife. What does he know of such things?"

John thought of his own large family and their home in Derryfield. He couldn't imagine squeezing any more people into the small farmhouse. His ma couldn't wait for them to be off and married. Yet everyone in Plaswa's house seemed to adjust to the inconveniences of living in a large group. Even his own presence, he had to admit, hadn't caused that much of a stir.

Plaswa finally returned. "The Council says you must work in the garden." He called to his wife and spoke to her in their own tongue.

Pidianske began to laugh, but she ran to get a hoe and gave it to John, giggling as she did so. Plaswa motioned for John to follow him. They walked past the church and through the center where the feast had been held. When they reached the bluff above the riverbank, Plaswa turned toward the huge gardens.

Women and young children were hoeing and weeding the crops. John was brought to a small field of corn. The tiny plants, just a few inches high, were planted in little hills. Weeds were already sprouting between the corn plants.

John saw a group of young men fishing in the river. He recognized some from the gauntlet ceremony. He saw Kasko, wading slowly, spear held above his head as he studied the water. And he saw Ogistin.

Ogistin looked up for an instant and stared at John. Then he began to point and laugh. Others in the fishing party joined in the merriment.

"What's going on here, Plaswa? What's everyone laughing at?" John demanded.

"I suppose they are laughing at you, John Stark."

"Why? They can't find me any funnier than I was two days ago. Ah, they're all talking about the fight and how I beat them. That's it, isn't it?"

"Perhaps." Plaswa yelled out to Ogistin and the others. Ogistin answered his uncle, and the others began to laugh once again. The women and children on shore joined in.

"All right, Plaswa. What joke are you telling? It involves me, doesn't it?"

"I put my nephew and the others in charge of guarding you, but he says the women should guard their own."

"What's that supposed to mean?"

"You are a clever man, Pastoni. You can discover the meaning to Ogistin's riddle."

After Plaswa left, John stood for a moment, leaning on the hoe. Then he began to hack at the weeds, glad to be doing anything requiring physical action. Occasionally a young girl would make a comment and giggle. John tried to ignore it.

He hadn't worked in a garden in years, except for plowing and turning the soil. He helped his pa with the heavy labor when he wasn't out trapping. His younger brothers and sister had been helping Ma with the planting and weeding since he'd been big enough to work with Pa and Will. Then it came to him: since he'd been big enough to work with Pa and Will...

So that's it, John thought. They aim to treat me like a woman! He wouldn't be allowed to hunt or fish or do any of the other work that were the men's responsibilities. He glanced at the other gardeners before he began to work furiously, going up one row of corn hills and down the other. As he worked, he thought about what he would say.

Everyone seemed to be too busy to laugh at him anymore. The women worked and chatted quietly. Some sang as they weeded. If any of the children noticed what John was doing, they didn't say. John looked at the small field. Perfect.

He turned toward the river and shouted: "Ogistin!"

The women and children in the garden stopped their work and looked at John, but the boy didn't look up. Ogistin was standing in the river, helping with some kind of reed net. So John tucked the hoe under his arm, cupped his hands around his mouth and yelled louder: "Ogistin!"

This time, he got Ogistin's attention, as well as that of the other fishermen. John hoped he'd say it right.

"Ogistin!" he shouted once again. He pointed to himself and said, "I am zanoba, ZANOBA, a *man!*" Then he shook his head and waved his arms. "Not behanem, NOT BEHANEM, not a *woman!*"

With that, John flung the hoe with all his might. It turned great circles in the air as it sailed down, then landed with a splash in the river, just beyond the group of fishermen.

John stormed away from the garden. He wondered how long it would take them to realize that he'd just hoed up every corn plant and left the weeds to grow.

22
A Call
to Bezo

O gistin grabbed the hoe as it floated by him. He watched John Stark walk away. "So!" Ogistin smirked as he spoke, "the Pastoni is not so stupid!" The other men in the group had watched the performance in silence. After a few seconds, someone began to laugh. Ogistin turned to see Missal chuckling to himself.

"Why are you laughing?" he asked.

"I was thinking...of...Simo!"

"What does this have to do with my brother?"

Ogistin wasn't sure he was happy to have his brother's name mentioned right now.

"Don't you remember?" Missal asked. "Of course, you wouldn't remember. You were just a baby!"

"Remember what, Missal? Tell me what Simo did that makes you laugh so."

"Why, he did exactly what the Pastoni did! Your mother brought him to work in the garden. It was his eleventh summer, I think—or his twelfth. No matter. But he threw the hoe in the river and announced that he was a man. He wouldn't do women's work! I was so impressed, I followed him!"

Now a chorus of chuckles and "Oh, yes, that's so!" and "I remember!" followed Missal's story.

Ogistin was confused. He absentmindedly touched the hunting bag. Simo? His brother had acted like the Pastoni? He waded to shore, dropped the hoe, and quickly climbed the bluff.

"The Pastoni are cowards and thieves," Toma had said. But John Stark was certainly not a coward. He'd lied to Plaswa to save his friends, and he'd fought to help them escape. Now he walked away from this work knowing full well, Ogistin was sure, that he could be punished for what he'd done.

Ogistin imagined Simo in the garden. Simo would have been praised for his action. It would have simply shown Simo's desire to become a man and take on greater responsibilities. Why had Ogistin been surprised that the Pastoni wouldn't allow himself to be treated like a child?

He walked past the gardens to the edge of the village and watched the Pastoni heading toward the center. Ogistin saw Plaswa in front of his cabin. The Pastoni wouldn't get far.

Ogistin turned and walked a short way from the village and found a quiet place to sit. He opened Simo's bag and removing the old lynx tooth, closed his eyes and called on Bezo, the cunning hunter, the secret-keeper. Ogistin pictured the lynx as he'd seen her just days before, in front of her den, staring up at the fox. Bezo's enemy was just a few yards from her cubs, yet the cat had made no move. Why?

Ogistin gripped the tooth tighter and tried to become Bezo, tried to picture himself watching the fox through golden eyes. Ogistin thought about the lynx cubs, safely hidden in their den. He saw the fox standing above, sniffing the air. Her little kit trotted easily behind her, unaware of Bezo. Ogistin stood motionless, just as Bezo had. In his mind, he stared at the fox, his whole body ready to spring. As he did so, he realized that he felt no threat. The fox picked up her cub by its scruff and bolted away.

The fox had been hunting for her kit. Bezo had just had a successful hunt. Each animal was interested in protecting what was hers, not looking for battle.

Why, Ogistin wondered, was he the only one who seemed to hate the Pastoni so much? Had he reacted to a threat that didn't exist?

Ogistin needed someone to help him sort out his thoughts. Someone wise who would listen and help him see what was right.

He put the lynx tooth back in his hunting bag, got up and went back to the village to find Atecouando.

23
Atecouando's Offer

ohn wasn't surprised when Plaswa said that Atecouando wanted to speak with him.

John was tired, tired from the work he'd done in the sun, tired of wondering what would happen next, tired of being a prisoner. But he walked behind Plaswa with his back straight and his head held high. He wouldn't show Atecouando how weak he was really feeling.

They met Atecouando as he was leaving his cabin.

The older man smiled at John and chuckled softly. He asked John and Plaswa to follow him to the river.

"It seems our young Pastoni does not like the work we chose for him," Atecouando said in English.

"I have been told," Plaswa replied.

John listened carefully, trying to determine if either man's voice held a note of anger. So far, Atecouando seemed amused. John couldn't tell anything from Plaswa's expression or voice. To make matters worse, Ogistin appeared from the other side of the church, walking directly toward them.

Atecouando called to the boy. John wasn't sure exactly what he said, but it was obvious that Atecoundo expected Ogistin to join them. Ogistin looks about as pleased as I am, John thought.

A small circle of logs had been arranged in the shade of a large pine tree at the edge of the bluff. There was a cool breeze from the river. They sat, and John found himself feeling relaxed in spite of his situation.

Atecouando, as usual, didn't hurry to speak. He allowed them all time to enjoy their pleasant surroundings. At last, Atecouando brought up the subject of John's earlier behavior. He spoke in English to John as Plaswa translated for Ogistin.

"You have little fear, John Stark," Atecouando said.

"Every man has fear, I think, Atecouando. I just don't always listen to mine, I guess."

Atecouando smiled and nodded, looking out toward the river as he spoke: "You have shown us many times that you are not guided by your fears, John Stark. There is much to admire in a man who confronts his enemies."

Atecouando waited only briefly before he went on: "I have decided to make you one of us, John Stark. You will have all the rights and privileges of one born in the village. We will teach you our customs and share what we have."

John sat quietly, waiting to hear more. He wasn't sure what Atecouando's words meant. Was this supposed to be good news? Should he be thanking Atecouando or should he be frightened?

"You will need someone to teach you our language and our ways," Atecouando continued.

John nodded, beginning to understand. He had heard that the Indians sometimes adopted their captives. "Plaswa could teach me," he suggested. John wasn't sure how he felt about being adopted, but he knew better than to argue.

"Perhaps later Plaswa will agree to carry on your training. But for now I think it would be better if young Ogistin worked with you. Ogistin needs to learn the Pastoni language if he intends to follow the hunters to Albany when they trade our furs."

John watched Ogistin's face change as Plaswa translated Atecouando's words. It was obvious, even to John, that while the boy was angry at Atecouando's decision, he wouldn't argue.

The Chief Speaker stood up to show that their visit was over. He said a few brief words to Ogistin and turned to walk back to his cabin.

"Atecouando thanks Ogistin for his help," Plaswa explained. "Ogistin will take you to the river to help with the fishing." Plaswa looked expectantly at his nephew.

"Wijawi, *Nijia*," Ogistin said with a stinging twist to his voice and turned toward the river.

Plaswa grinned and said to John, "It seems my sister's son takes this responsibility very seriously. He says, 'Come along with me, my *brother*.'"

24
Ogistin
the Teacher

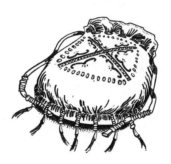

The Pastoni followed Ogistin into the river, pausing only to remove his leather boots and throw them on the riverbank.

Ogistin rejoined Missal, Kasko, and the others, feeling as if he were being trailed by an unwanted dog.

"What's he doing?" Kasko asked, gesturing toward John Stark.

"Atecouando wants him to help us," Ogistin answered, not ready to tell his friend the whole truth.

The Pastoni stood in the river watching Ogistin. Ogistin wondered how to explain the work of re-weaving the broken weirs to someone who didn't speak his language. The weirs were reed-and-stick gates placed in the river. Water could flow through, but fish were held back, making it easier to spear them. The swift-flowing river weakened the weirs so that they had to be regularly checked for damage. Kasko and the others had come today to remove the broken ones and repair them.

Ogistin lifted one of the weirs and showed John Stark where spaces had become large enough to allow fish to pass through. The men took several of the weirs back to shore.

Missal handed Ogistin some thin wood strips to replace the broken pieces. Ogistin wove one through the spaces and then gave the materials to John Stark. The Pastoni's hands moved clumsily, and after a few awkward tries, the fish trap looked as bad as before.

Ogistin tried to show John Stark again, but the Pastoni did no better. He held the weir too tightly and only managed to make the spaces even larger.

"You'd better have your grandmother teach him with a mat or basket first," Kasko said. "I don't think he's ever woven anything before."

"I think you're right," Ogistin said, "but what can I do with him?"

"Give him a spear. He can't break anything while

he's fishing," Kasko answered.

Ogistin smiled. There were several fishing spears stuck in the mud at the river's edge. He grabbed one and motioned John Stark to follow him upriver where a few of the other men were standing quietly, ready to spear the migrating fish.

Ogistin found a good spot below a trap and motioned for the Pastoni to stand still. He raised his spear and watched the river carefully. Minutes passed before he plunged the spearhead down and brought up a fat, struggling fish. He pulled his catch off the spear and threw it to Kôgôwés, who had a basket strapped to his back.

Ogistin held the spear out to John Stark, but as the Pastoni took it, he slipped and fell backwards into the river. Ogistin and the others laughed as John Stark scrambled to his feet, spitting and shaking his head furiously, sending great splashes of water around him in a circle. The spear he held was cracked. John Stark looked at the broken pieces in surprise.

That made Kasko and Ogistin laugh even harder. The Pastoni smirked in embarassment. The harder the others laughed, though, the harder it was for him not to grin, and suddenly John Stark was laughing at himself with the rest.

PART III
Six Weeks Later

25

News from Montréal

ohn hadn't been easily convinced that Ogistin would honor Atecouando's request. But things had started to change after that day at the river. It had been difficult at first. John and Ogistin had watched each other for the slightest sign of threat.

Was Ogistin trying to make him look foolish again, John wondered, or did the men really tend the tobacco plants? Did the Pastoni really not know how to build a canoe, Ogistin asked himself, or were his mistakes done to slow the work?

It surprised Ogistin that John Stark had never made a boat and would have bartered for one instead. John learned that the men *did* take charge of the tobacco. The plant was considered sacred and grown in a separate garden.

Eventually, John could understand nearly everything that was said to him, but he still had some difficulty speaking the language. He and Ogistin communicated in sentences mixed with English and Abenaki and even some French words.

One of the first English words Ogistin learned to say was *why*. Ogistin wanted to know the reason for anything John did differently.

"Why do Pastoni leave behind the bones of the animals they catch?" Ogistin asked him.

"What good are they?" John asked in return. "I'm not about to make soup in the middle of the woods."

Ogistin explained the Abenaki custom of thanking the animal for giving its life, and then he added, "That's how we found you and your friends. You left many bones behind. Even the hunting animals don't leave so much."

As the two men worked together, Ogistin continued to question John. Why do Pastoni men walk in such loud shoes? Why do you wear hats when it's not winter? Why does each family plant its own crops? Why not share what you have?

John tried to explain as best he could, but since he now wore the cooler summer clothing of the Abenaki, he wasn't sure there were good reasons for his tall boots or any hat. He felt so much more comfortable in the vest and breechcloth and short summer moccasins.

John told Ogistin about his pa's farm and the reason Archibald Stark had come to New England.

"It's important for a man to have something he can call his own," John had said. "If Pa had stayed in Ireland after he married my ma, everything he worked for would have belonged to the Crown."

Ogistin had scoffed at that. "Our leaders do not keep things for themselves. A good leader sees that his people have the things they need. If your king is too selfish then you should name a better one."

Though Ogistin asked many questions during this time, more often he would say nothing, and John would find Ogistin quietly watching him, studying him.

On the night of the naming ceremony, many of the villagers gave John gifts to help establish his new life among the Abenaki. John was amazed at their generosity, but Plaswa explained that giving a gift was a serious matter. Ogistin's gift was the most surprising: his beautiful quilled hunting bag with its fire-making kit and medicine pouch.

"Take it," Ogistin had said. "It is all I have left of my brother, Simo. Someone once told me that you acted like him. I have seen that it is true. You and Simo *are* alike in some ways. For this, it is good to call you Nijia."

With the naming ceremony complete, John was treated as a son and brother. He left Plaswa's house and went to live with Azô and O'nis instead.

He spent the summer weeks learning about the people of St. Francis. He fished and tended tobacco; he helped cut timber for a new cabin.

He gradually came to see differences among the villagers of St. Francis. For though they now considered themselves one People, they maintained pride in their various heritages. Atecouando still carried a knife his Pennacook grandfather had given him when he was a boy. O'nis kept special possessions in a birch container etched with Pigwacket pictures, which once belonged to her grandmother.

John was shown the difference between Micmac designs and Pasamaquoddy designs in quillwork. He knew Penobscot baskets were prized for their sturdiness and tight-fitting lids.

From Plaswa and Ogistin and Azô, John mastered more knowledge about survival in the woods. He learned to wait longer, to take only what he needed, and to need less. John now understood why the English had such difficulties in their wars with the French and Indians. The British army, in their bright red uniforms, still fought in the European manner,

lined up like so many toys. The king's soldiers came to America expecting the Indians to adjust to these European rules of warfare. The Abenaki taught John to blend in with his surroundings by wearing the colors of the trees and the animals.

And always, as the villagers shared their knowledge with John, Ogistin was nearby, helping, working, and watching.

One day, several weeks after the naming ceremony, John and Ogistin were walking out of the woods after a short hunt. Ogistin pointed to one of the rabbits in John's hand.

"Mali will want that one," Ogistin said. "She makes fine boots and will want the dark fur for trim."

"She's welcome to it as long as she cooks the meat for me," John said. "Your sister makes the best rabbit stew I ever tasted."

"Try to tell her that, Nijia. She does not like to cook. She would always rather make clothing. She usually trades work with Talaz. You probably ate Talaz's stew without knowing it."

The two hunters laughed.

"Well, whoever makes that stew can have these rabbits," John said.

They reached the river and turned toward St.

Francis. Ogistin saw the canoes first. "Atecouando
is back," he said, gesturing upriver.

Atecouando had been to Montréal to meet with the
French Governor. As Chief Speaker, it was his func-
tion to visit with the Governor several times during
the year. This time, Kasko had gone along. John
knew Ogistin was anxious to see his friend and hear
about the trip.

They jogged to Azô's cabin, left the rabbits with
O'nis, and ran back to the bluff. In seconds, they'd
hurried down the bank and were ready to help unload
the canoes. Some of the men quickly hauled trade
items up to the village center to display or give to
the owners.

Kasko was unusually talkative. Montréal was larger
than he remembered. There were more people than
he could count. They hadn't had any rain either, and
everything was very dusty. The French king across
the ocean had a new son, so the city was celebrating
the birth of the prince.

Kasko and Ogistin went up the bank to join the
others. John was about to follow, when Atecouando
stopped him. "Stay, Nijia. I must speak with you,"
the older man said.

They climbed the bank in silence, and walked to
Atecouando's cabin. Atecouando's wife brought
them bowls of soup. The two men sat quietly
sipping and watching others greet the returning men

and examine the trade goods. John didn't question Atecouando, although he was very curious. He was learning patience.

Finally, the old man said, "We spoke with Phinneas Stevens from your colony. He searches for Pastoni prisoners and pays their ransoms."

John looked up, startled. "What are you saying, Atecouando? Have they paid for me?"

"You are not a prisoner, Nijia. You are Abenaki now. You may come—or go—as you please."

John sat quietly thinking, I've known the truth for some time. Why didn't I leave?

He knew the answer. He hadn't been unhappy in St. Francis. He'd been treated well and learned so much. Even if he'd been able to find Amos, he couldn't have paid for his release. But Atecouando's news jolted him. The Chief Speaker was giving him the opportunity to make up his own mind. Atecouando was showing John exactly how much freedom the naming ceremony had given him.

John put down the bowl. "I have to find Ogistin," he said.

Kasko and Ogistin were sitting in front of Azô's cabin talking and laughing.

"Nijia!" Ogistin called when he saw John. "Come and hear about Kasko's trip."

John decided to tell Ogistin immediately. "They're ransoming English prisoners in Montréal."

Kasko nodded. "Gamelin, the mill owner, has agreed to free your friend."

John turned his head sharply. Atecouando hadn't told him this part of it. Maybe the old man had wanted him to make his own decision about leaving or staying without worrying about Amos. But if Amos were going too...

Ogistin was studying John's face. "Will you go, Nijia?" he asked.

John sighed. "Look, even 'adoption' can't make me one of you, Ogistin," John said solemnly. "We both knew I'd leave someday."

Ogistin put down his bowl. "What did you think your naming ceremony meant? Didn't you see the others who live in our village? Père Aubery, and Rachel, Nespaouit's wife—they are Abenaki now, just as you are. Why would you want to leave?"

John turned to Kasko, but his eyes held the same questions. John stood up and shook his head. He untied the beaded bag and gave it to Ogistin. "I have been proud to wear this," he said. Then John walked back to tell Atecouando he'd be ready to leave for Montréal whenever he was given the word.

The canoes were loaded for the return trip to Montréal. This time, Toma and Lobal would also accompany the group, going on to Albany to trade the furs that had been taken during the Long Hunt.

John stood on the bluff, feeling hot and itchy in his old clothes. His feet already ached in his boots.

All the time that John and Amos had been forced to march to St. Francis, John had thought about home. He'd imagined heading south through the White Hills to Derryfield. Even during his first days in St. Francis, he'd dreamed of the day he would walk beyond the boundary of the village as a free man. But nothing had come close to what leaving St. Francis was truly like. He'd have never believed that leaving might be hard. He was heading north again, but this time, going north meant he was going home. And, oddly, he felt as if he were leaving friends and family behind again.

Plaswa came to say good-bye. He wouldn't be making this trip to Montréal, but he brought John's musket and hunting knife. "We do not return you to your English family defenseless and starving, John Stark."

"And don't forget these, Nijia," said another voice behind John. Ogistin held the three beaver pelts.

John smiled. He hadn't expected Ogistin to come see him off. John took the beaver pelts. "These hardly seem worth the fight we had the day I set the traps." he said.

Ogistin grinned. "It was a good fight." He took

the knife and sheath that hung around his neck and presented them to John. "Do not forget your time here," he said.

John took Ogistin's knife and hung it around his own neck. "You have been a good teacher," he said, putting the knife Plaswa had returned to him in Ogistin's hand. He touched the young hunter's arm and then turned to walk down the steep hillside to Alsigôtêgok. As John stepped into the last canoe, the party pushed off, paddling quietly. The river breezes were pleasant, but he faced away from them to watch St. Francis disappear.

Ogistin straddled the top of the bluff until the canoes went around the river's bend.

"Perhaps you'll see John Stark again," Plaswa said as he turned to go.

Ogistin only smiled at his uncle's comment. He gripped the Pastoni knife, thinking he'd learned more in the last few months than Plaswa or Atecouando or even his mother would have guessed. He felt like the lynx, the cunning hunter, the secret-keeper. If he ever met any Pastoni again, he would know how to put all his knowledge to use.

Epilogue

John met Amos in Montréal.

Captain Phinneas Stevens and Major Nathaniel Wheelwright had been sent to Montréal by the Massachusetts colonial government to ransom English colonists. By the time John Stark arrived, the Frenchman, Gamelin, had already accepted sixty pounds sterling for Amos and another colonist, Seth Webb.

Since John wasn't considered a prisoner, the Abenaki wouldn't accept a ransom for him. But Mr. Stevens gifted the St. Francis men with a pony for which he had paid five hundred and fifteen pounds.

The group returned to the British colonies by way of Albany, New York, where the St. Francis Abenaki completed their fur trading. Amos and John arrived in Derryfield in late August of 1752. Will Stark had made it home too, and the brothers were reunited.

One of the first things John did upon his return was to go trapping—to repay the Massachusetts colony.

It would be nice to think that because of the time John Stark spent in St. Francis, relations between the British and Abenaki would have changed, and both sides would have become friendlier. Unfortunately, this wasn't the case.

British and French colonists, helped by the Abenaki and other Native American allies, continued to fight each other over control of the colonial lands. By 1759, the colonial British government was tired of more than eighty-five years of "Indian troubles," as they called them. They assigned Major Robert Rogers and his Rangers the task of destroying the village of St. Francis. The British were convinced that most of the skirmishes originated from this mission village.

On the morning of October 4, 1759, Major Rogers and his forces crept into the sleeping village. They shot and killed many people (even though they'd been ordered not to harm women and children), and set the houses afire. They took some women and children as prisoners.

Major Rogers claimed to have killed over two hundred Abenaki. French observers, who arrived after the attack, noted only about thirty dead, *mostly* women and children. But this much is certain: after Rogers' Rangers were through, only three storage buildings remained standing. Stories and songs still tell of the destruction of the village and the murder of the St. Francis Abenaki.

Atecouando survived Rogers' attack. His name appears on a letter written ten years later to British Governor Guy Carleton complaining about whites using Indian land.

Throughout the years, many strong young women

and men, like the fictional Ogistin and Kasko, helped their people and culture survive the continuous European immigration. It is estimated that the Abenaki and their descendants now number in the tens of thousands in Canada and the northeastern United States.

John Stark was a captain in the Rangers at the time of Rogers' raid. But he was not among the men who marched to St. Francis. Stark had been sent, with two hundred other Rangers, to build a road through the Vermont forest. History doesn't record his feelings about the attack, but one Stark historian feels that John would have found it detestable.

John Stark's grandson, Caleb Stark, wrote of him: "In the latter days of his life, he used to relate with much humor the incidents of his captivity; observing that he had experienced *more genuine kindness* from the 'savages' at St. Francis, than he ever knew prisoners of war to receive from any 'civilized' nation."

John Stark learned firsthand about war with "civilized nations" when he became an officer in America's war for independence from England. This time, John's brother became an enemy. Will Stark chose to side with the British Loyalists.

In 1822, Major General John Stark died at the age of ninety-four. He was the last surviving general of the Revolutionary War.

Glossary

Many of the Abenaki words used in this book were taken from Abenakis and English Dialogues, *by the Abenaki scholar Joseph Laurent (Sozap Lolo). Most of the remaining words are from a new dictionary of the Abenaki language being revised by Gordon Day and Jeanne Brink. I have labeled the words with an L or D to credit the appropriate source.*

Agat (ah-GAHT) Abenaki version of the name Agatha [*L*].

Alsigôtêgok (ahl-sih-GOHN-tuh-gok) the St. Francis River [*D*].

Atecouando (ah-teh-kwah-HON-doh) Jerome Atecouando was the Chief Speaker—Orator—for the St. Francis Abenaki from 1749–1757. The name Atecouando means "Deer Spirit Power" [*D*]. (Some of Atecouando's words in this story have been taken from actual speeches and historical documents.)

Azeban (ah-zuh-BAHN) Raccoon [*D*].

Azô (ah-ZOHN) Abenaki version of the name John [*L*].

behanem (pah-HAHN-uhm) woman [*D*].

Bezo (PEEAH-zo) Lynx or Bobcat [*D*].

Gici Niwaskw (gih-shih-nih-WAS-kuh) God; literally Great Spirit [*D*].

Kasko (KAHS-koh) a heron [*L*].

Klalis (kuh-LAH-lis) Abenaki version of the name Clarissa [*L*].

Kôgôwés (kohn-gohn-WEES) meaning saw-toothed person [*D*].

Kokokhas (koh-koh-kuh-HAHS) Owl [*L*].

Lobal (loh-BAHL) Abenaki version of the name Robert [*L*].

Mali (MAH-lee) Abenaki version of the name Mary [*L*].

medawlinno (muh-dah-wah-LIHN-noh) a person with power, a sorcerer [*D*].

Missal (mihs-SAHL) Abenaki version of the name Michael [*L*].

Nespaouit (nehs-PAH-wiht) name of a St. Francis man from near the time of 1752 [*D*].

nijia (NIH-jih-uh) my brother: a term used by men. A woman would call her brother nidobso [*L*].

nokemes (noh-KEE-muhs) my grandmother [*D*].

nzasis (n-ZAH-sihs) my uncle (mother's brother) [*L*].

Odanak (OH-dah-nahk) a village [*L*].

Ogistin (OH-gihs-tihn) Abenaki version of the name Augustus [*L*].

O'zalik (ohn-zah-LIHK) Abenaki version of the name Angela [*L*].

O'nis (OH-nihs) Abenaki version of the name Anna [*L*].

Paslid (PAHS-lihd) Abenaki version of the name Basil [*L*].

Pastoni (pahs-toh-NIH) A Western Abenaki word for Bostonian [*L*].

Patlihôz (PAT-t-lih-HONZ) priest, pastor of a church [L]. (Père Aubery was an authentic member of the St. Francis community in 1752.)

Pidianske (pih-dih-AHN-skeh) Penobscot woman's name.

Plaswa (PLAS-wah) Abenaki version of the name François (Francis) [D]. (Plaswa was a real member of the hunting party that captured John Stark.)

Sazal (sah-ZAHL) Abenaki version of the name Caesar [L].

Talaz (tah-LAHZ) Abenaki version of the name Theresa (Thérèse) [L].

Toma (toh-MAH) Abenaki version of the name Thomas [D].

wampum (WOM-puhm) small beads made from shells and used by many North American Native American cultures as money or jewelry [D].

Wôkwses (wohn-kuh-wuh-SEHS) Fox [L].

zanoba (sah-nohm-BAH) Abenaki word for man [D].

For Further Reading

Baldwin, G. C. *Games Of The American Indian.* New York: Grosset & Dunlap, 1969.

Bruchac, Joseph. *The Wind Eagle and Other Abenaki Stories.* New York: Bowman Books, 1985.

Bruchac, Joseph. *Return of the Sun: Native American Tales from the Northeast Woodlands.* Freedom, CA: The Crossing Press, 1990.

Bruchac, Joseph. *Fox Song.* New York: Philomel, 1994.

Calloway, Colin G. *The Abenaki.* New York: Chelsea House Publishers, 1989.

Crompton, Anne Elliot. *The Ice Trail.* New York: Methuen, 1980.

Cwiklik, Robert. *King Philip and the War with the Colonists.* Englewood Cliffs, NJ: Silver Burdett Press, 1989.

Deur, Lynne. *Indian Chiefs.* Minneapolis: Lerner Publications, 1972.

deWit, Dorothy (editor). *The Talking Stone; An Anthology of Native American Tales and Legends.* New York: Greenwillow Books, 1979.

Epstein, Anne M. *Good Stones.* Boston: Houghton Mifflin, 1977.

Giffen, Daniel. *The New Hampshire Colony.* New York: Macmillan, 1970.

Pike, Robert E. *Fighting Yankee.* New York: Abelard Schuman, 1955.

Putnam, George. *Old Number Four.* Orford, NH: Equity Publishing, 1965.

Richmond, Robert P. *John Stark, Freedom Fighter.* Waterbury, CT: Dale Books, 1976.

Voight, Virginia F. *Close to The Rising Sun: Algonquin Indian Legends.* Champaign, IL: Garrard Publishing Company, 1972.

Whitehead, R. H. and H. McGee. *The Micmac: How Their Ancestors Lived Five Hundred Years Ago.* Halifax, N.S.: Nimbus Publishing Limited, 1983.

Wilbur, C. Keith. *The New England Indians.* Chester, CT: The Globe Pequot Press, 1978.

A Note of Thanks

No book of historical fiction can be completed without the help and cooperation of many people. For this reason, I would like to thank the following:

Jeanne Brink, whose Abenaki grandmother grew up in Odanak. Thank you, Jeanne, for acting as "expert reader" and commentator as well as sharing the Abenaki language with me. The hours you spent on this project will always be appreciated.

Gordon Day, for his input and suggestions based on his years of study of the people and language of Odanak.

Jacques Use, of the Société Historique d'Odanak, Réserve Indienne des Abénakis: Merci encore pour votre temps, votre connaissance historique, et votre reserche de tous mes questions.

Richard Boisvert, archaeologist and supervisor of fieldwork for the New Hampshire Division of Historical Resources, and Charles Miner, Wildlife Biologist for the New Hampshire Fish and Game Department, for sharing their expertise.

Betty Lessard and Kathy Staub, of the Manchester Historical Association, for their help and support.

Sally Wilkins, Jane Buchanan, and Kathy Deady, who were in on the project from the beginning and were willing to listen to endless revisions.

Paul Stevens of the Abenaki Labor Council; Deny Obomsawin of Odanak; Stephen Laurent (son of Joseph Laurent) and owner of the Abenaki Indian Shop; Michael Caduto, author of *Keeper of the Earth* and *Keeper of the Animals*: you all helped lead me to the right sources.

Carly Bordeaux, native consultant, for her insightful critique.

Marybeth Lorbiecki, editor, for her constant and unfailing encouragement.